D1548222

Evangeline

ENDORSEMENTS

Evangeline is a beautiful delineated story of love and courage, right and wrong, and how we all have the chance to make a difference in this world. Lane Jordan sincerely allows you to fall in love with every chapter. A delightful read.

—**Liz Morris**, The Dallas Dream Team President, Personality Doctor

Anytime I read stories in the Bible, I imagine what it would be like reading their adaptation in a contemporary context. Therefore, I was delighted to read the story of Evangeline.

Lane Jordan has done a brilliant job in this adaptation of the story of Esther, which talks about God's divine intervention and deliverance of his people—the children of Israel—in times of hopelessness and despair.

In *Evangeline*, the author gives a very well-researched account of some of the events that took place during the civil rights movement of the sixties in various parts of the nation and skillfully integrates them into the story of Evangeline—the modern-day Esther.

I encourage you to take time to relax, to read, and to digest the contents of this beautiful book. It will be life changing!

—**Omokorede Fasoro**, ILO Certified trainer, writer, speaker, and personal discovery coach.

Evangeline is a tale of love, fear, prejudice, and power. In every generation, power-hungry schemers emerge who try to manipulate hatred to increase their own dominion, regardless of the bloodshed. Lane Jordan cleverly weaves the Old Testament story of Esther into the racial conflict of twentieth-century America.

—**Lisa Worthey Smith**, best-selling and award-winning author, *The Elijah Mandate*

Nehemiah 7:5 says, "So my God gave me the idea ..." There are numerous good ideas, but occasionally, there is a God idea. I believe this brilliant work, *Evangeline*, by Lane Jordan is the latter. In a world often divided by color, culture, and class, she provides a unifying voice offering Kingdom perspective by reimagining and modernizing the timeless narrative of Esther. The story is creative and captivating and the truth transformative, leading us to truly seeing each other as God does and loving one another.

—**Jelani Lewis**, Gateway Church, Plano, Texas Campus Pastor.

Evangeline

LANE P. JORDAN

PUBLISHING THE POSITIVE
Plymouth, Massachusetts

Copyright Notice

Evangeline
First edition. Copyright © 2021 by Lane P. Jordan. The information contained in this book is the intellectual property of Lane P. Jordan and is governed by United States and International copyright laws. All rights reserved. No part of this publication, either text or image, may be used for any purpose other than personal use. Therefore, reproduction, modification, storage in a retrieval system, or retransmission, in any form or by any means, electronic, mechanical, or otherwise, for reasons other than personal use, except for brief quotations for reviews or articles and promotions, is strictly prohibited without prior written permission by the publisher.

This is a work of fiction. Names, characters, businesses, places, events, locales, and incidents are either the products of the author's imagination or used in a fictitious manner. Any resemblance to actual persons, living or dead, or actual events is purely coincidental.

Cover and Interior Design: Derinda Babcock
Editor(s): Peggy Ellis, Deb Haggerty

PUBLISHED BY: Elk Lake Publishing, Inc., 35 Dogwood Drive, Plymouth, MA 02360, 2021

_____

Library Cataloging Data
Names: Jordan, Lane P. (Lane P. Jordan)
Evangeline / Lane P. Jordan
194 p. 23cm × 15cm (9in × 6 in.)
ISBN-13: 978-1-64949-369-9 (paperback) | 978-1-64949-370-5 (trade paperback) | 978-1-64949-371-2 (e-book)
Key Words: modeling, beach read, biblical story of Esther, racism, New York, friendship, family
Library of Congress Control Number: 2021946056 Fiction

DEDICATION

To every person of color or race who has been thought of as 'less than.' You are not. You are created souls in the image of God. May we remember God's greatest commandment: To love one another.

ACKNOWLEDGMENTS

"No man is an island" is certainly true when writing a book.

I would not have the time or the emotional fortitude to write without the caring and support from my husband, Scott, along with all his technical support.

To my AWSA and CAN sisters who consistently pray and support each other.

To Deb Haggerty—Elk Lake Publishing—and her amazing staff of talented editors.

Peggy Ellis, thank you. This book became special with your help and input.

To all the ladies in my Bible Study and Life Group who prayed for me, especially Lisa Gillman who helped with fashion descriptions.

To my precious daughters Christi and Grace, and granddaughter Sara, whose love and friendship give my life fullness of joy.

And to my Lord God, who has given me abundant life on earth and eternal life with Him. I am blessed indeed.

PROLOGUE

1949

I don't remember much about that freezing December night. I do remember being woken by my Meemaw. Her soft touch and words were unusually tender. She pulled me from my warm covers toward her large bosom, holding me so tightly I could hardly breathe.

She looked right into my eyes. "You gotta go on a trip with Uncle Martin, and you gotta be brave, very brave."

As I blinked my eyes awake, I looked around the small shack. My cousins were crying. "Where's Ma and Pa?" I asked.

Meemaw offered me a slight smile. "Why, they've gone through the door to the other side. But it's not your time yet, so we gotta let you go ... go to safety."

"But I don't want to go! I don't want to leave you and our home and ..." I looked down at my kitty, who had wrapped herself in a ball by my feet. "I don't want to leave Kitty."

"Now listen to me, my precious Hattie. This here is dangerous times. Your Ma and Pa, well, they tried to keep away, but it finally caught up with them. Now, we've already packed up your bag. You're going on a train trip—won't that be fun?"

She laid her hands on my head, prayed a blessing over me. "Never forget that God is like the wind—invisible but always with you. Remember who you are and where you came from, dear child. Remember all those who love you dearly. Live a life of truth, kindness, and love. Every hour of your life is important, for *you* is important! Be strong, be courageous, and be brave. Don't never, ever forget where you came from."

I don't remember much else but crying for my Ma and Pa. Someone put my coat and hat on me while I sobbed. My uncle pulled me from my Meemaw and carried me to the wagon that was already horsed up in the dirt yard. The horses started moving immediately after he set me in the back on some blankets.

That was the last time I ever saw my home or my dear, dear Meemaw.

CHAPTER ONE

Evangeline. What a great name for a model. For the first time in fifteen years, Hattie—who had become Evangeline immediately when they'd moved to New York from Mississippi—was disappointed her uncle had insisted on the change. Even now at eighteen years old, she still didn't care much for her new name, but she had grown accustomed to it as well as calling him Mr. Martin rather than Uncle Martin. He'd reminded her many times over the years to never, ever let anyone know he was her real uncle. With her starting a new school at such a young age, he had to remind her often.

Even now, Uncle Martin and Evangeline still looked over their shoulders. Fear pervaded their thoughts. The men who killed her parents had tried to follow them as they hurriedly left her home, but Uncle Martin had avoided them. He thought New York, with its millions of people, would be a great place to hide. He still got reports from friends and relatives that the men were not giving up. They were looking for a black man and a white child in every city. That was why Martin insisted from the moment they arrived in New York that Hattie become Evangeline, that she forget he was her uncle, and that she become a different person with a different background. He didn't know then how long the deception would last. Still didn't.

Now, as the taxi meandered through the streets of New York, Evangeline realized again how wonderful the city was—

the Empire State Building, Fifth Avenue with its extravagant stores, the fame and glory of Broadway, Rockefeller Park where she ice skated with her school friends, and Times Square where she wasn't ever supposed to go.

Finally, she had her first apartment in the best city in the world. Margie, Evangeline's best friend, was already there when she opened the door. They squealed with laughter and ran around the large living room before finally collapsing on the sofa.

"Isn't this the best apartment New York has ever had?" Evangeline asked.

"None like it. The world is our oyster, but we have to get jobs." Margie held up a newspaper. "Let's look at the Help Wanted ads."

"I'm not to that point yet. My first stop is the Ford Agency. I already have my résumé and letters of recommendation from school. All I've ever wanted to do is model, as you well know. I found out today I have an appointment tomorrow."

Margie squealed with delight. "That's great! I know you'll get the job of your dreams."

Evangeline looked out the window. The view from their Fifth Avenue apartment was spectacular. She could even see Central Park. She'd been overwhelmed when her Uncle Martin had decided to settle in New York City. The skyscrapers, throngs of people, and constant noise had made her homesick initially—to the point of crying herself to sleep most nights. Thankfully, she'd met some wonderful new friends, had great teachers, and lived in a loving atmosphere at the boarding house. Eventually, she learned to love the city and to realize all she could experience and accomplish here—the art and natural history museums, libraries, and Ellis Island with the Statue of Liberty. Last year, a group of her friends went to Kennedy Airport and saw the Beatles getting off the plane.

Her uncle had sent her to a boarding school, and afterward, a Fashion/Modeling school because of her desire to be a model. He supported himself by working at King's Department Store, starting as a janitor, and moving up to head of security. It was a good job and gave him a good life. As long as he could always look after Hattie/Evie, he was happy. Evie was grateful for everything he had done for her, but now she wanted a taste of freedom.

She knew the type of person the Ford Agency wanted. The envious title of "Ford model" brought its own reputation. People recognized Ford models as the top of their profession with legs that stretched for miles, lots of blonde hair, tall, and that extra ingredient—eagerness, enthusiasm, and sparkle that spoke volumes of what these models were capable of. They were the best of the best. The crème de la crème.

Evangeline had been told all her life how beautiful she was. She wasn't quite sure. Her skin was way too white to be as pretty as her mama's face had been, but she was taller than all her friends. Her best asset, apart from her height, glowing skin, and high cheekbones, was her hair— honey blonde, exceptionally long, wavy, and very thick. She hoped it would be her ticket to the runway.

"Margie, I'm going to the Ford office first thing tomorrow for that interview. I'd love for you to come with me."

"I don't have the right look. You go ahead," Margie said. "I'm going first to King's Department Store. People say it's the up-and-coming new store, patterned after Selfridges, the wonderful store in London. Your Mr. Martin told me how wonderful this store is. I'd love a job in their fashion design department."

"Good thinking. That was your best subject at school. Let's go out now and celebrate our jobs. You know we'll get them."

The doorbell rang. Rushing and giggling to be the first to open it, Evangeline yanked open the door. Her Uncle Martin was standing there, smiling, and holding several suitcases.

"I guess these belong here, huh?" he smiled as he stepped inside and set the suitcases down, then went back to the hallway for a large trunk. "What do you have in all of these, Miss Evie? They weigh a ton."

"Oh, just my necessities. Thanks so much for bringing everything here. I can't believe I'm finally on my own, Mr. Martin," Evangeline said.

After he had brought everything in, he looked around. "You done good, Miss Evie. This looks like the best apartment in all of New York City."

The girls fell on the sofa laughing. "That's what we said too!"

Martin smiled with a twinkle in his eyes.

"Oh, I just remembered. I have one more box for you." Martin went back to the hallway and brought in a small, cardboard box which he handed to Evie.

"What's this, Mr. Martin? No presents, remember?"

"I know, but this is something special. Go on and look inside. You too, Miss Margie."

As Evie gently pulled back the top of the box, light filtered through to show a small, round, soft lump. She reached down and touched it and when she did, a tiny, pink tongue slipped out of a small mouth, showing a great big yawn.

"A kitten! Oh, Mr. Martin, a kitten, for me?"

Martin laughed. "Yep. I remember you had to leave your kitten way back when we left Mississippi. I thought now was a good time for you to get another, seeing you got your own place now. Do you like her?"

Evie pulled the sleepy kitten to her chest. "Oh, it's the best present in the world. Thank you, thank you! She's just beautiful. Look, Margie."

Margie reached out to stroke the kitten's soft fur. "She looks just like a little princess, doesn't she? I'm already in love with her too, Evie."

"Princess. Yes, Margie, that's the perfect name. She'll be a princess and will rule this apartment like she owns it." And the girls erupted in gales of happy laughter which made Martin flash a megawatt smile.

"Well, I do love to see my girls happy, yes I do. I also brought her litter box and kitten food, but you might want to get her something pretty to sleep on."

"Yep, she can sleep on a pillow on my bed. Oh, Mr. Martin, I'm so happy."

"So, what are you girls going to do tonight?"

"We were going out to celebrate our new jobs at some restaurant. No, we don't have them yet, but we're optimistic! Now, I think I just want to stay home and play with Princess. What do you think, Margie?"

"I agree. Nothing can be as much fun as playing with a new kitten."

Mr. Martin smiled again. "I'm glad you'll be staying here. You're used to the safety of the school. So, when you do go out, remember to be careful. I'll go now. You two enjoy your new apartment and your new roommate."

Margie was the first to speak after he left. "Evie, I've known you for years now and I've been wondering ... where did you get all the money for this kind of apartment and where on earth did you find Mr. Martin?"

Evangeline sat down on one of the velvet wingback chairs facing the fireplace, holding the kitten, now asleep, in her lap.

"You really want to know?"

"I really want to know."

She thought for a moment to make sure she explained it the way Uncle Martin had coached her. "It's funny because I don't know a great deal myself. I only know my daddy's parents in Mississippi were extraordinarily rich. Had one of those plantations with the large white-columned front porches, lots of land, and lots of people working for them. When they died, I was the only one left in the family, so everything came to me.

"You already know my mother and father died when I was very young. I still don't know how. Mr. Martin worked for my grandparents, so he brought me to New York City.

Said it would be safer for me here. Not sure what he meant by that. He found the boarding school where I met you.

"Every Saturday, he'd take me for lunch in the King's Tea Room where I got to see the fashion show. I usually sat by myself, but sometimes, I could bring a friend. Remember some of the times you came?" Before her friend could answer, Evangeline continued. "Oh, those models were so pretty. And they would always stop at my table and say hello and smile special at me. I used to pretend one of them was my mama. That's when I started dreaming of one day becoming a model."

Trying to hold back a tear, Evangeline looked at Margie.

"I've had a wonderful life, Margie, but I don't think anything would be as good as having a real family to live with and to love. That's really my main desire, even more than becoming a model. Maybe one day, I'll have a husband and children."

"Oh, Evie, you'll get that—I just know it. No one is as kind and loving as you are. And with Princess, you can start practicing right now."

CHAPTER TWO

The next morning, Evangeline stood on her patio, drinking coffee. She purposefully chose this room facing due east so the sun would wake her each morning. She loved seeing the brightness of a sunrise, enjoying the early morning smell of a new day, and watching people going to and from work or school as they walked on the sidewalk. She was one of those Pollyannish people who saw life in a positive way. Today was no different as she contemplated her future. If the agency rejected her, she'd just go to another one. She would not be persuaded to give up her dreams. She also knew she needed to pray before she even got dressed—to ask God for peace, wisdom, and discernment.

An hour later, Evangeline took a taxi to the Ford Agency. As she looked up at the impressive building, her stomach flipped. But she held her head high as she walked into the beautiful and well-appointed lobby. She would remember who she was, just like Uncle Martin had told her Meemaw said she should. No one could defeat her.

"Hello!" Evangeline said to the receptionist at the glass and marble counter. "I have an appointment today. I'm Evangeline Emerson."

The woman, who was so skinny her clothes must have been holding up her body, looked Evangeline over, and without even a smile, asked her to fill out some paperwork.

Evangeline was so busy concentrating on the paperwork she didn't hear the door to the agency open. However, she did hear the receptionist tell someone to leave.

Looking up, Evangeline saw a shabbily dressed figure clutching a bag and asking for something to eat or drink.

"Go away!" exclaimed the sour-faced girl behind the desk.

As the figure began to leave, Evangeline hurried to her. "Hello, can I help you?"

A twenty-something-year-old girl looked up at her and didn't say anything. She just shuffled toward the door.

"Please, I'd be happy to get you some water. Wait here."

Evangeline looked over at a table with paper cups, a water pitcher, and a coffee maker. She poured some water into a cup and brought it over to the tiny figure.

"Here you go." She handed her the cup of water. "What else can I do?"

"Thank you, I'm OK. Just needed something to drink." She headed for the door.

"Does that happen often?" Evangeline asked the receptionist as the young woman left.

She shrugged. "New York has a lot of homeless people. Some of the homeless women think we're supposed to help. Don't know where they get that idea."

Evangeline went back to filling out the paperwork but couldn't concentrate. How could women not have a place to live?

Soon, the door opened, and another young lady called her name. "Is there an Evangeline here?"

"Here I am." Evangeline raised her hand just like in her school days.

"Please come this way." She led Evie down a beautifully carpeted hallway. "Wait inside this office. Eileen will be here shortly."

Evangeline couldn't believe her good luck. Eileen Ford herself would interview *her*—a little girl from backwoods

Mississippi. Evie's palms started to get sweaty, and her chest tightened. She reminded herself to breathe. She had heard Eileen was a very domineering lady, strong-willed, and opinionated. But before she could bolt, the door opened revealing a dark-haired woman smaller than Evangeline had thought she would be. And though not a beauty, she had a kind and warm smile.

"Hello. I'm Eileen Ford." The woman reached out her hand to shake Evangeline's. "You must be Evangeline. I've heard so much about you."

"Hello. Thank you, but from whom?"

"Oh, I have my ways." She laughed. "I know the headmistress at your school. Her recommendation is what got you this interview."

"Well, that's good news. Mrs. Ford, I've wanted to be a model since I was old enough to eat lunch in King's Tea Room where I would see the beautiful models. Once I could read, I started looking at fashion magazines. I've loved all aspects of the fashion industry. I've heard the Ford Agency is the best. In fact, I've heard you and your husband transformed the modeling business in the process of creating a new caliber of fashion models. So, thank you for taking the time to interview me. This really means so much. By the way, everyone calls me Evie."

"OK, Evie, tell me all about yourself. What type of goals do you have?"

Evie filled her in on her background, starting with her move to New York as a young child, followed by boarding school, then the fashion school. She also shared her desire to be a model as well as to be active in the fashion industry in other ways.

"Well, all I can say is, after reading your résumé and now meeting you in person, I'd love to welcome you as a model for us."

"Really? Oh, I can't believe my good fortune. I can't thank you enough." Evie jumped up and started shaking Mrs. Ford's hand.

Mrs. Ford chuckled. "Do you have a place to live? Many of my models live with Jerry and me in our home—our way to help the girls acclimate to big city life, as well as give their parents less to worry about. New York can be a scary place at times."

"Thank you, but I have an apartment and a roommate, so right now I won't need your help. I'm glad to know I could move in with you if I had to."

"Then let's get you started. I'll have my assistant bring you the paperwork to sign, and then, she will show you around. We're having a staff meeting at one o'clock today, so please join us, and you will be able to meet everyone."

Eileen left the room, and the next few hours were filled with signing papers, meeting people, going to the fitting room to be measured, having headshots made, and attending the staff meeting. By five, when the office closed, Evie felt she'd been to a whole new country. Everything was new and wonderful. As soon as the headshots were finished and sent to the ad agency, her first jobs would come in. She hoped.

Evie was so excited she didn't even hail a taxi but, instead, hurried home to share everything with Margie. She wasn't disappointed, and Margie was there with her own exciting news.

"I got a job at King's Department Store!"

"I got a job at Eileen Ford's Agency!"

Both girls hooped and hawed and jumped up and down. Finally, they fell on the sofa with squeals of joy.

"Oh, Evie, I'm so happy for both of us. To have jobs already is too much to take in."

"I know, Margie, I know. A lifelong dream has been fulfilled. I can't wait to take you to see the agency. Everyone is so nice and wants to do everything they can to help me. They've already taken my headshots. Soon, I'll have my first modeling job—maybe even a runway or a magazine layout."

"You deserve this great opportunity. I can't wait to take you to King's. Even though you've spent so much time there, I bet you haven't been in the back rooms where all the real action takes place. I'll work with the design team—assist with the store design and decorating, work with the new fashions coming in, and design the windows. I may even get to help with the fashion shows, and if I do, I'll see you, Evie."

They started laughing and giggling all over again. Princess's meows joined their laughter until Evie settled the tiny kitten in her lap where she soon fell asleep under Evie's caressing hand.

"Oh, and I saw Mr. Martin. Since he's the head of security, he made sure all the paperwork had been given to me and signed. He said one day I'll meet Mr. King himself."

"Now that would be a day to hope for!"

CHAPTER THREE

ONE YEAR LATER

"Margie, can you help me find my silver cloak? I know I had it here just a moment ago. I need it for my modeling job at King's Tea Room."

Evie's modeling career was doing well. She wasn't modeling couture yet, but she did catalog ads for Sears, Roebuck and Co., as well as some runway shows. Although the Fords were strict in what the girls could eat, what they could do, etc., they were fair, honest, and found jobs for the girls. Evie loved every job she went on. Of course, she was still doing some of the smaller ones like the Tea Room today, but size didn't matter. She was part of the fashion world of New York City, the fashion capital of the world. One day, she knew she would get more exposure, either in a magazine ad or a couture runway show.

She had already met some of the more famous models at the Ford Agency. During her first month at Ford's as she got on the elevator, a beautiful girl asked for her name.

"Evangeline ... Evie. I've just started with the agency."

"Oh, you will love Eileen and Jerry. I started with them, too, and they have helped me out of some horrible financial problems. My name's Suzy Parker. My sister, Dorian, got me an interview with them and here I am. I hope we run into each other again."

Margie held out the cloak. "Here. You must have laid it on the kitchen counter when you were getting something to eat."

"Thanks so much. I'm extra excited about my job today because the MC for the show is King's fiancé, Vanessa. I've heard so much about her but have only seen her one time at the store. Have you seen her?"

"Not face to face, but she's everywhere at the store. You wouldn't believe the pull and power she has over every department, especially with the fashion and design. One day, I was in one of the windows, arranging our new window display, and she casually walked in, pulled one dress out and put another one on the mannequin, smiled, and left. The funny thing is the dress she added was the perfect one. She has that touch and flare. I hope you get to meet her."

"I do too. I've heard that since she arrived, the store has become even more luxurious. You can get practically any item you could ever want."

"The store has changed—more expensive items and hard to find ones are showing up in all the departments. Vanessa travels the world each year buying specialty and rare items. I'll try to see you at the Tea Room on my break."

"Great. I'll look for you."

Evie grabbed her purse and cloak. As she rode the elevator down to the lobby floor, she thought about how her life had changed over this last year. She had been a girl looking for work after fashion school, and now she worked for the best modeling agency in the world. She loved her apartment, her roommate, and living in New York.

She made sure she said hello to Davis, the doorman, and left her building. She marveled at the ability of architects and engineers who built such skyscrapers. How could these buildings not fall over? The thought made her laugh as she made her way down the street.

The long-stemmed flowers were in full bloom and waving in the gentle breeze on this sunny morning late in May. The grass smelled freshly mowed and a food-cart's grilled onions made her mouth water. People were sweeping in front of their small stores that lined the street, and the park was full of young children playing hopscotch and enjoying the swings and slides. Yes, the summer heat would soon be here, but Evie didn't care. New York, hot or cold, winter or summer, was her town. She didn't know how life could get any better.

She arrived early at the store and gave herself a few minutes to look over some of the glass counters filled with every beautiful item a heart could desire—crystal decanters filled with rich perfumes, sterling silver writing pens, soft leather clutch bags and gloves. As she turned toward the elevator, she saw Vanessa going that way. My, she was pretty. Maybe if she hurried, she could get on the same elevator. As Evie started to speed up, a stock boy with a load of boxes in his arms crashed into her, and both fell to the marble floor.

"Oh, miss, I'm so sorry! Are you all right?" the boy said.

As Evie looked up, Vanessa smiled and reached for her hand.

"Are you OK?" she asked. "Here, let me help you up."

Evie was embarrassed but moved her feet and legs around and realized she was all right. She stood with the helpful hands of Vanessa and the red-faced stock boy.

"Oh, thank you. I'm fine. Just a little shaken. Let me help pick up the boxes."

The stock boy stopped her and said he would, so the two ladies went to the elevator.

"That was a nasty fall," Vanessa said as the elevator carried them upstairs. "I do hope you're all right."

"Truly, I'm fine. Thank you for helping me. Oh, I'm Evie—one of your models for the fashion show in the Tea Room today."

"You did look familiar to me. I've seen you before as a model. So happy you aren't hurt and can model today. Well, here we are on the third floor. I'll see you later. Nice to have met you."

Evie parted ways with Vanessa, wishing they had met under better circumstances. Maybe someday.

As she opened the door to the models' area, she caught her breath at the beauty of the chaos before her. Models walking around wearing gorgeous outfits; hairdressers fixing hair; makeup specialists doing three girls' makeup at one time; and someone shouting something but no one apparently listening. Yes, this was heaven.

As Evie got dressed in a beautiful floral shirtwaist dress, she realized, though she had just met Vanessa, she had met Mr. King while looking for a graduation dress in his store. After that meeting, Uncle Martin said Mr. King was a remarkable man and a great manager of all his employees. Maybe he would be at the fashion show. She also hoped Martin and Margie would be able to break away from their jobs to watch her.

The show started without a hitch. The lights came on, the crowd of lunching ladies hushed, and Vanessa stepped into the spotlight.

"I'm pleased to welcome each and every one of you to one of New York's finest department store and fashion shows, King's!" Vanessa smiled and waited for the applause to end.

"I personally selected the collection for this show. The theme? 'Let's travel to a faraway place.' Sit back and imagine yourself far, far away in the most beautiful designs ever created."

The lights dimmed, and one strong spotlight revealed the first model, showcasing a full-length, white mink coat.

The audience applauded.

"Yes, you will have to stay warm as you cruise the Queen Elizabeth on your way to Europe," Vanessa said.

The applause assured Evie this would be one of the best shows King's had ever presented. Each design Evie wore seemed to be loved more than the one before it. The cash registers would be busy today.

As Evie hurried back to her station for her last gown, Vanessa's assistant came running holding a white gown.

"Evie, the model who was going to wear the wedding gown has just gotten sick. I need you to put the gown on right now. You will be the last model to go out in about two minutes."

Evie looked at the dress she held—the most stunning dress she had ever seen. Lace and pearls covered most of the white satin fabric on the bodice which displayed a delicate and tasteful low neck. The long sleeves came to a point on the back of her hand. The train was exceptionally long and edged with the same lace and pearls as the dress. As the assistant pulled up and fastened the gown, Evie felt like she was a bride. The hairdresser brushed her long hair then placed a tiara on top, added some diamond earrings, and a short, solitaire diamond necklace—at least five carats.

Evie took one last look in the mirror. Never had she worn anything this magnificent. She felt like a queen.

"Hurry, Evie, hurry! Vanessa is ready to call for this number."

The spotlight lit on Evie's face as she reached the stage. Without hesitation, she stepped onto the red-carpeted runway, inwardly smiling at the wonderful comments and excitement from the audience.

When she got to the end of the runway, there right in front of her was Mr. King himself dressed in a beautiful suit and tie with his dark, full hair brushed back. He was so handsome. She froze mid-step as he smiled at her. She lowered her gaze, made a successful turn on the runway, and headed back to the front of the stage. The models paraded the runway one last time to wild applause as they presented the most coveted designs at King's.

Margie and Martin waited for her in the models' area.

"Oh, Evie, you were wonderful," Margie said. "You looked like a princess or queen or angel up there all in white. I was so proud of you."

"Yes, you did, and I'm also very proud of you, Miss Evie." Martin smiled.

Quiet fell in the room when Mr. King came in.

"Mr. King, I don't think you've met Evangeline Emerson—the child I've been entrusted to take care of while she lives in New York."

"Thank you, Martin, for introducing us." King gazed straight into her eyes. "Hello, Evangeline. You did a wonderful job today presenting the bounty of our exclusive designs. But we have met before, remember? You were in the ladies' dress department looking for a graduation dress."

"How ... how did you remember that? I'm flattered." Evie looked away as she said softly, "You can call me Evie. Everyone does."

"Then Evie it is. How long have you been a model?"

Evie took a deep breath to calm her nerves. "Almost a year. As soon as I finished school, Elaine Ford hired me. Modeling was a dream of mine, and I've loved every minute."

Mr. King laughed. "You should be immensely proud of yourself. Eileen Ford is picky, so if she chose you, then you have a great career in front of you. Now please excuse me, I'm needed elsewhere."

He hesitated before he left and took both of her hands. "May I say again, Evie, seeing you again has been a pleasure. Martin, you were not exaggerating about her modeling capabilities ... or her beauty!" Then he was gone.

Evie shook her head in disbelief. He had held her hands, and he had remembered them meeting. Her heart flipped.

After Margie and Martin left, Evie changed clothing and went back to the agency, but everything was in slow motion. Never had anyone affected her the way Mr. King had. She knew without anyone telling her she must get over those feelings quickly.

CHAPTER FOUR

During the next few weeks, there was a buzz all around the store—King's Department Store would host two grand banquets on the same day.

"Evie, have you heard Mr. King will have banquets that will outshine the word 'banquets'?" Margie asked one night after work. The girls were enjoying a rare night at home. They had cooked dinner and were now lounging on the sofa playing with Princess and her ball of yarn.

"Then the rumors are really true? Two banquets on the same day?"

"I heard the first banquet will be for couples, men and women. And the second banquet will be separated—one just for the men and one just for the women, so I'm sure Vanessa will have a fashion show. I bet you'll get to be a part of all this. Isn't this going to be historic?"

"Without doubt. I've got an idea. I'll visit you at the store tomorrow, and we'll get Mr. Martin to show us where the rooms will be. What do you think?"

"Evie, that sounds perfect. And while we're there, I can show both of you the design plans for the two banquets. It's going to be one crazy time for the next few months. Mr. King wants the banquets in November. I hope it all comes together."

The next day, Evie came to the design offices, picked up Margie, and walked to Mr. Martin's office.

"Hi, Mr. Martin," the girls greeted him. "We're here to see where these landmark banquets will be. And look." Margie held up a rolled-up document. "The design department has started on some ideas. Let me know what you both think."

"Good to see you two. First, we'll go over to the second floor where there's space that used to be for storage."

When they got to the second floor, Martin opened two double doors to reveal a large but empty room.

"The design team, can do just about anything they desire," Martin said. "Look over there." They walked to the other side of the room and saw an open-air patio. "This patio has been here as long as this old building has been standing. Mr. King wants to have gas torch lights all around the area."

"He wants to decorate the room and the porch as luxuriously as possible. Look at what we've decided on so far." Margie laid the blueprint plans on the floor. Magically, the room was transformed into a palace in their minds. "Mr. King wants to import the finest silks from India and the Middle East to cover the three walls over here. He wants the patio to look like an enclosed garden with hangings of white and blue linen, fastened with cords of white linen and purple silk attached to silver rings on marble pillars coming from Italy. The border of the garden will have lit torches as well as stone-lined pathways, marble benches trimmed in gold, countless pots of flowers, and tables for all the different foods he wants created."

"Oh, Margie, really? I can't believe he's going to such expense. Bring the blueprints over by the window so we can see better. Explain what you'll do to the main room. I can't imagine how to fill such a huge space," Evie said, and Mr. Martin agreed.

"Yes, the room is quite large, but David, the head of our design department, has some great ideas. He divided the room into three sections. See the division lines? The first part will have plenty of velvet couches, trimmed in gold and silver with gold tables dispersed between them, with plenty of gold ash trays. On both sides of this first section will be gorgeous gold tables where the caterers will place the appetizers and drinks. I heard him tell the chefs he wants so much food and wine available that no one will go thirsty. The wine will be served in crystal and gold pitchers. I even heard Mr. King talked to the head chef about the wine selection. He wants each bottle displayed and a label with name and year next to the bottle. They will also have every type of crystal glassware you can image for every type of drink. Can you even believe all this?

"The second section will have the tables for the actual meal. Mr. King has requested beautiful silks to cover these tables along with gold chargers, gold flatware, crystal glassware edged with gold, and gold candle sticks. He wants us to import oriental rugs to cover the floors and the same silks to cover the walls. I'm sure we will add spotlights and lots of candles. Lighting is so important. Of course, the actual food planned will be over the top. The plan is for the attendants to file out of the kitchen single file to show everyone all the exotic items and then they will serve the guests.

"The head table, always the largest, will be in the last section of this huge room. Mr. King will invite the most important people to his table."

"Who will he invite?" Evie asked.

"I don't know but, Mr. Martin, you will probably get the guest list before anyone to help you manage security."

"You're right about that. I'm waiting for that list to arrive any day. My, is this going to be a nightmare. Fun. But a nightmare."

Evie and Margie laughed. "Might be a nightmare for you, but heaven for us."

"Mr. Martin, the plans for this area are beyond belief. Now, can you show us the room for the ladies' banquet?"

"Come this way. We don't have any more room on this floor, so we have to go up to the third and the room is kinda hard to find." After going up another staircase, Mr. Martin went down a hall that had lots of doors. "As you can see, this used to be office space, which we don't use anymore, but at the end of the hall—just look."

He opened the doors to a room that was perfect for the ladies. The large room was in great condition with beautiful inlaid hardwood floors.

"Oh, Margie, I had no idea King's had so much extra space. Do you have the plans for this room with you?"

"No, we haven't gotten that far. Planning every detail is going to take a long time. I'll let you know as soon as we have the plans in print."

They left the room, lost in their own thoughts about the spectacular event being planned and hoping Mr. King would get exactly what he wanted.

The first of November came with cooler temperatures, but the sun was warm on her face. As much as Evie would have loved to enjoy the weather, her main concern was getting to King's Department Store to go over the last-minute preparations for the ladies' banquet and fashion show. Just nine more days. As they had anticipated, Mr. King's banquets were causing a media sensation. Never in the history of the city had a business planned such elaborate and expensive banquets or parties.

Through these last few months, Margie continued to tell Evie every detail about these banquets especially some of the 'who's who' King had invited—every top official in New York City, as well as Governor Rockefeller—to come to what he called, "The Banquet of a Lifetime." In addition to politicians, he had invited important businessmen and heads of states from all around America and the world. His goal? To make King's Department Store as famous as possible.

Finally, Margie got the plans for the ladies' banquet and asked Evie to come to the store as soon as she could get away from the Ford agency.

"Evie, the ladies' banquet room will be even more gorgeous than the first room. Look at these plans. Vanessa kept them a secret, so I just now got to see what the room will look like. The workmen are putting the room together as we speak. She worked closely for weeks with our department to get exactly the look she wanted—a fantasy or magical room.

"Every wall, sofa, chaise lounge, chair, and table will be covered in the palest silks with a blush-pink hue. String quartets and harps will play throughout the evening. Vanessa ordered chandeliers to hang from the silk covered ceiling, and throughout the room are trees with tiny lights. And flowers will be everywhere. She wanted to add as much magic and beauty as possible. Look at this part of the room. A runway for the fashion show. On each side of the runway will be thousands of white roses in gold urns. Evie, you'll get to be a part of this beautiful event."

As Evie looked at all the details, she realized this would be a landmark event. She couldn't wait.

As Evie got off the elevator on the third floor the Monday before the weekend of the banquets, one of Vanessa's assistants called to her.

"Oh, there you are, Evie. You got here early, thank you. We want all the models to be comfortable with these fashions before the big day. All of us are frantic with this whole spectacle. What if something goes wrong?"

"Let's calm down. The only thing that has to be perfect is the food and wine." Evie grinned. "If the women consume enough wine, no one will notice the food."

"We all would benefit from your perspective. Come on and let me show you the gowns you'll wear for the fashion show."

The assistant led Evie to clothing rod after clothing rod of finery of all descriptions. She found her name attached to one of the rods and began trying on each outfit. The other models soon joined her with exclamations about their own outfits.

"Why is Mr. King going to all this trouble?" one of the models asked. "This so-called 'party' is going to cost him a small fortune."

"Because he intends King's to be the best department store in the world," answered a strong voice. Vanessa, wearing a Chanel suit and matching pillbox hat, strode into the room, a smile lighting her face, looking more beautiful than ever. "Nothing will stop him if he showcases the rare merchandise his store is known for and brings in the most important people—the rich and powerful. His reputation for knowing where to buy exotic items and how to display them will be unsurpassed. He will truly be 'King' in the arena of fashion and marketing." She glided away, leaving the models feeling especially important that they would have a part in this historic event.

Evangeline was thrilled to be one of the models selected for the lady's banquet fashion show, which would be the highlight of the evening for this historical day. Even Margie had an important project from the design department, and Mr. Martin had brought in extras to help with security. The place was a madhouse.

When Evie saw Uncle Martin across the room, she headed over to talk to him.

"Hi, Mr. Martín. Are you ready for the big day?"

"Good to see you, Evie." He motioned a clipboard toward a half dozen men standing with him. "Do you know my top security heads?"

"I've met each of you from time to time. So nice to see all of you again."

"We're going over our plan again today," Uncle Martin said. "King insisted we enlarge our security. We've never had a situation like this with so many outsiders coming into the store at one time. There will be cooks and waiters and florists and designers from all over the world. Some don't even speak English. I've decided to put a different head of security over each of the different areas, and he has permission to hire as many people as he needs. I will be over everyone, and with our walkie-talkies, I believe we'll be OK. From now until the ninth, we'll work together until we know the schedule and our placement by heart."

Evie asked, "Mr. Martin, can I speak with you a moment?" They walked to a quiet alcove. "Do you think someone from back home might use this opportunity to look for me?"

"You read my mind, Evie. Just know I'm not letting anything get by me just in case."

"Thank you. I know you'll keep an eye out for both our safety. I need to get back to work myself. Hope you have a good day."

She returned to finish going over each outfit, what time she would wear each, and the complete order of the night. She could hardly wait to see some of the invited guests. American socialite and style icon Babe Paley, wife of CBS founder William S. Paley, who was named to the International Best Dressed List Hall of Fame was coming with her other socialite friends, Slim Keith, C. Z. Guest, Gloria Guinness, and Pamela Churchill. They were so famous they had a nickname: The Swans of Fifth Avenue. And of course, Babe would bring her absolute best friend, Truman Capote. At least Evie hoped so because she loved his *Breakfast at Tiffany's* which she'd read in her high school English lit class. Maybe she would have a chance to meet him.

Margie shared that Mr. King had invited the top tier of every type of occupation—financial leaders from Wall Street, lawyers, law enforcement, government officials, as well as at least a dozen of Hollywood's elite including Rex Harrison, Julie Andrews, Sean Connery, Lauren Bacall, James Stewart, and John Wayne. And to outdo even himself, he invited leaders and kings from many of the world's nations. One such world leader was the Prince of Monaco and his beautiful wife, screen actress Grace Kelly.

It would indeed be an occasion never witnessed before or, probably, ever again.

CHAPTER FIVE

Finally, the day of the Great Banquets was here. Evie and Margie arrived early to watch the dignitaries as they entered the store. They were able to get a good spot on the sidewalk near the elaborately decorated front entrance. That's when Evie noticed a young woman who looked familiar, standing close to the side of the building but slumped over.

"Hello! Are you OK?" Evie asked her.

"I'm fine, just hungry," the young woman said. "I recognize you. You got me some water one day in an office building."

"Yes, I'm Evie and this is my friend, Margie. Are you homeless? Can we help you in some way?"

"I'm not homeless all the time. I work a little here and there. But the paycheck just doesn't last long enough for food. I decided to come and look at the festivities."

The whole city of New York was in a complete state of excitement and confusion. People lined the streets, hoping to catch the sight of someone "important." Those who had been lucky enough to get an invitation had been boasting and prepping for this day for months.

"I'll tell you what. Take this card up to the restaurant on the top floor. They will get you something to eat." Evie took a pen out of her purse, wrote her name on her card, and a note telling them to help the woman. "With all the activities in the rest of the store, a restaurant has been set up to feed all the workers and the security men. Give them my card. I hope you'll get enough to eat."

At first, the woman wouldn't take the card, but Evie and Margie finally convinced her. Evie had an idea.

"Monday, after all this is over, come by and ask for Mr. Martin. He's a friend, and I'll tell him to expect you. I'll ask him if he has a permanent job for you at King's. What's your name?"

"Oh, thank you so much. My name is Anna. You have no idea how much I've struggled." She wiped tears from her eyes. "I'm really hungry. Thank you!" She headed into the store.

"That was hard to witness," Margie said. "I can't believe people are really homeless in our city, though I hear about them all the time. But to see one—especially a woman—makes me so sad. Thanks for helping her. Do you think she'll get hassled because she's colored?"

"I think she'll be fine since she'll be eating with the workmen and security. OK, let's go in the store ourselves so we can see everything."

Evie and Margie had hardly slept a wink the night before, staying up late reviewing everything they were supposed to do the next day. Martin had eaten dinner with them before he had to go back to the store. He'd decided to bring in a camp cot and spend the night at the store. There was too much security that had to be checked and rechecked for the next day.

The girls were glad they arrived at the store early. They would see all the action, as well as escape the inevitable traffic jams. The first banquet was at noon but the guests had been asked to arrive early. By ten-thirty, the limousines were stacked back-to-back, letting off their important and well-dressed occupants.

As Evie and Margie climbed the front marble stairs towards the large main double-door entrance of King's, they could barely walk without tripping on the white roses overflowing the gold and silver urns. Magnificent swags of fabric and roses hung over the double-doors and windows. Inside, Evie gasped.

"Margie, this looks like a scene from *Lawrence of Arabia*. See the draped silks on the walls and the large cushions? And over there, they even placed palm trees and giant urns with flowers."

"You're right. I can't believe how authentic King's first floor has been transformed into paradise. Do you think we can even find the elevator? Perhaps we need to take the grand staircase up to the second floor. We can look down and see the whole floor.

"I love seeing all these rich and important people." Margie said as she peered over the banister. "I wish we could see into the beautiful banquet hall. I've helped some with the designs but I haven't seen the final decorated room. All I know is the room will be impressive."

"I have a great idea," Evie said. "I'm sure Mr. Martin would let us into the security room, and we can view everything through the widescreen security cameras."

The girls hustled to the next-floor security offices. Sure enough, they slipped in unnoticed. The guards were busy watching the screens and talking to the ground crew. Evie and Margie could see the dignitaries coming into the newly decorated banquet room and the magnificent décor and table settings. Then they saw Mr. King's arrival.

"I think he's kind of into himself. What do you think, Evie? Everyone in the design department tried to tone down his ideas but Mr. King wouldn't budge."

"I know what some people think, but for some reason, I think Mr. King's a good guy underneath all this pomp and circumstance. At least I hope he's not that narcissistic. Mr. Martin really likes and respects him and told me he's done so much for other people. I believe he's trying to make sure when people think of fashion and merchandise, they think of King's, not him."

Evie had heard stories about King, his past, his interests, and work ethic.

The tall, elegant, refined, and very wealthy man had made a name for himself in the retail and business world of New York. He became an orphan as a teen and realized he would have to make his own future. While in high school, he worked in the shipping and receiving basement warehouse for Marshall Field's in Chicago, and soon learned the business.

He was self-taught about business but also studied the biography of every entrepreneur he could. He believed by studying those who had already become successful in the retail world, he could apply those insights to his own life and the future store he wanted for himself one day.

Evie also heard that King had studied men such as Harry Selfridge who started Selfridges in London as well as the men who started Hudson's in Detroit, Macy's, Marshall Field, Lord and Taylor, and even Rich's in deep south Atlanta. He was able to glean from all their great ideas and make his store even better. As Harry Selfridge proclaimed, "Shopping should be a pleasure activity, and the customer is always right."

Sure enough, although he wasn't yet thirty-five, King's store was one of the finest on the East coast if not the whole country.

King was also well-read. He realized, that without attending college, he would have to be his own professor to earn a Bachelor of Arts degree. Along with biographies, he read every book he could get his hands on about science, history, medicine, engineering, architecture, master artists, and even space. He eventually developed connections with NASA and was confident America would be the first country to reach the moon.

He loved books so much he became a passionate collector of rare, first editions, especially those by twentieth-century American authors. William Faulkner, F. Scott Fitzgerald, Robert Frost, Harper Lee, John Steinbeck, and Ernest Hemingway were some of his favorites. He had created a very impressive library in his townhouse and even had some of his favorite books in his office at King's.

He appreciated a disciplined life. He got up each day at the same time; arrived at his store exactly thirty minutes before the store opened to welcome and encourage his salesforce; held meetings with his staff weekly; ate his meals in the well-renowned King's Garden Restaurant and Tea Room; and enjoyed meeting and dating beautiful women. He lived in a stately townhouse not far from his store. He furnished his home with antiques and pieces he bought as he traveled all over the world looking and buying rare items for his store.

After living through his sad childhood, he knew a man's real strength was in his character, his value system, and how he treated his fellow man. Though he was known to date many beautiful women, he wanted to marry an exceptional woman and have a family. He believed Vanessa was that person.

The girls were glad they had decided to come to the store to watch the festivities. They weren't needed until evening for the women's banquet, but they couldn't keep away from seeing such an historical event. For the next few hours, as they sat transfixed looking at the sights below, they marveled at how the room had been transformed from an empty warehouse on the second floor to a room fit for a king. The walls now covered with beautiful silks had large canvases of famous oil paintings on them, including an original Monet water lily.

The whole ceiling had also been covered in fine silk with chandeliers hanging every few feet. Along with lit candles on every surface, the chandeliers gave off a soft and warm glow, showing off the dark mahogany tables.

The girls could see assorted toasts being given and the overloaded trays of food being carried throughout the room. Each chef from around the world came to the main room, introduced himself, his country, and the specialty item he had made. Gold and silver trays offered all types of fish and meat, including venison, beef, chicken, pheasant, lamb, and even more exotic fare. Customers and dignitaries could enjoy escargots de Bourgogne, an alligator with his mouth open "eating" a cooked chicken, a whole pig with the head included and an apple in its mouth, oysters, weiner schnitzel, and delicacies from China, Thailand, and India, as well as from Europe.

The fruit trays had every type of tropical fruit, as well as familiar ones—apples, oranges, and grapefruits. One tray even had exotic fruits most people would have never seen: plantains, kumquats, kiwano melons, mangosteen, and snake fruit. And plenty of trays included dates, figs, and raisins, as well as every vegetable one could imagine. The display was a spectacle they were sure they'd never see again.

"I don't know about you, but I'm already exhausted," Evie said. "Let's walk home and take a nap before the Ladies' Dinner tonight. If we don't rest now, we won't get another chance till early in the morning."

"You're right, Evie. We need to rest but I'm also worried."

"About what?"

"I don't know exactly," Margie replied as they quietly left the store through a back entrance. "I love this store, and I hope everything goes well tonight."

CHAPTER SIX

"Quick, we better hurry and get back to the models' area," Evie said. "I need to be dressed for the fashion show because Vanessa wasn't sure when she wanted us to walk out. She mentioned the fashion show might go a little differently than she planned. Her assistant would be doing most of the work. I also hope we get something to eat. Do you think there will be any food for us?"

After the girls had rested and changed into their nicest dresses, they hailed a taxi back to the store. Since they had arrived early, they had the chance to put away their wraps and purses and head back to the second floor so they could view the spectacle again.

Sure enough, the important dignitaries, stars, and wealthy patrons began to arrive. They were dressed so over-the-top Evie and Margie laughed. One man even had a wrap of lion skin—with the head still on. Women had crowns, tiaras, and capes trimmed in ermine over their long and glittering ball gowns with beautiful jewels adorning their necks and arms.

"They'll have food trays for us backstage," Margie said, "but I really want to see how the women's banquet room is decorated for tonight's gala. Let's run in there quickly before the ladies arrive."

The girls hurried to the third floor and down the carpeted hallway where they found the ladies' banquet room, opened the doors, and realized that nothing could have prepared them for what they saw.

"Evie, I saw some of the design drawings for this room, but nothing on paper revealed this beautiful room. The décor—everything—is unbelievable."

Before them lay a sparkling, silver, gold, and rose-colored, magical room. Spotlights were placed in specific places, lighting up the seating areas along with chandeliers glowing with soft, dimmed light. Flowers and their fragrance were everywhere but camouflaged so they appeared to grow from the floor. White and gold flowers seemed to sprout from the center of every table, cascading down the sides. The ceiling had been tented with linen and silk, festooned with fairy lights like strings of pearls. Silver and gold apples covered an apple tree. Even some doves appeared to fly overhead.

Colored lights dappled the walls and fell on the rows of brocaded divans, couches, and chairs. A violinist and harpist tested their instruments, playing little runs and trills. Golden cages filled with songbirds hung from the tent's posts and peacocks strolled around in one partitioned area. On one side, golden tables contained tray after tray of delicacies and desserts—cakes with sugar flowers melted on each layer, bowls of chocolates for dipping, and bakery foods too numerous to count.

On the other side of the room, more tables groaned under the weight of tempting foods. Delicacies from every corner of the world were displayed—everything from a roast pig embellished with a customary apple in its mouth to exotic fish to roast tips, and veal, pork, and poultry.

"I've never in my life seen such a sight," Evie said. "This must be what heaven looks like. I'm sure the ladies will be here any second. I need to hurry to the backstage area and get ready for the fashion show."

Chaos reigned in the fashion models' dressing room. Everyone knew how important tonight was to Vanessa, to their future as models, as well as to Mr. King.

They could see into the ladies' gorgeous banquet hall through a window in an upstairs loft overlooking the whole room. They just had to walk up a few steps from the backstage area. Evie had been so overwhelmed when she initially saw the room she hadn't noticed how the dining tables had been decorated.

These tables for the women were overloaded with gold and silver plates, utensils, flowers, and gifts at each place setting. The unique floor plan kept the room from being crowded. Vanessa had placed all the tables for the banquet in the center of the large room, leaving the first section for talking and mingling.

This first area was filled with small silk-covered tables with crystal glasses and punch bowls so no one would stay thirsty for long. The floor was covered with bright, oriental rugs in colors of rich maroons and indigo that gleamed with silk and contrasted beautifully with the blush-pink color theme throughout the room. Chandeliers hung every four feet so a bright but beautiful light flowed throughout the room, and Vanessa had placed candles everywhere. At the end of the room was the catwalk for the fashion show, each side lined with containers filled with thousands of white and blush roses.

"Look, Evie, even the attendants are styled in Arabian clothing, and they have jewels on their foreheads. See the flowing robes, silk trousers, and the turbaned swamis?"

"Yes, but, Margie, look at Vanessa's gown! A work of art for sure."

Evie had heard Vanessa leaned in her clothing tastes to those of Jackie Kennedy's skirt suits and pillbox hats. So, for this important ballgown, she went to the first lady's designer—Oleg Cassini. Her dress was in the same blush-pink tone she'd used throughout the enchanted room. The gown had a tight bodice, full, romantic skirt, close-fitting waist, and a low décolletage. Customized details could be seen everywhere on the dress—small white pearls and sequins sewed on the bodice, tiny silver ruffles along the back and in the pleats at the waistline, and they sparkled when she moved. Darker rose-colored sequins and diamante jewels were scattered all over the train.

"Oh, Evie, have you ever seen such a dress? It looks almost like a wedding gown."

"I think I'm too dazzled even to speak," Evie said. "This dress should go in the Smithsonian Museum for sure."

Each banquet seat had the woman's name on a gold card. Attendants helped the women find their place at their table and presented them with the present Vanessa had already chosen personally for each guest. These gifts had been beautifully wrapped in gold satin fabric and silver bows.

As each woman opened her gift, you could hear the ooh's and screams of delight as they held up necklaces, bracelets, and chandelier earrings, along with beautiful scarves or capes to show their friends. A lot of thought had gone into each gift, and the women were delighted.

Evie thought even King Solomon with all his wealth couldn't have had a room this beautiful or gifts so wonderful, even when the Queen of Sheba had visited him.

Evie could hear the music coming from the musicians playing softly in the background and remembered one of the violins was a Stradivarius. They also saw platter after platter of unidentifiable delicacies taken to each table. Though the food tables were set up as if to be a buffet, no one had to leave their seat as the attendants took care of each guest with all the food and drink they could want. Attendants brought desserts on rolling carts, even the chocolate fountain.

All too soon, one of Vanessa's assistants called out to them. "Models, you need to get in formation. Remember, the Givenchy blue velvet formal gown starts the show tonight."

Evie hurried with the rest of the models, excited that the show was finally beginning. As she found her position, she saw Vanessa leave the room through a back door. Where was she going right when the show was beginning? Evie hoped there wasn't some emergency.

Evie focused her attention on her job when she heard the countdown. The music came on, and the fashion show began.

During the women's festivities, the men were having an elaborate banquet also. There was even more food, wine, and liquor than they had experienced at the first banquet, and because this one consisted only of men, they enjoyed the spirits much more. Probably a little too much.

As the evening progressed, King looked around and was quite pleased with himself. He began to think of his future and how well Vanessa would fit into his life. She was not only beautiful but smart. She even seemed to want to be co-equals with him, as evidenced by her sitting in on every meeting. Her opinions and ideas were superb. She seemed to be a modern-day King Midas, for everything she was a part of turned to gold.

She had an eye for design and color that few possessed. Without interfering, Vanessa was able to give subtle hints to the designers of the floors and windows, ideas for the next floor design, and generally, was a huge help in the buying of the couture from France.

When influential women came to shop, they were sent to her, and before the day was out, they had armloads of bags and boxes from the most expensive sections of the store. The match of the king of department stores and his queen seemed to be made in heaven.

I know what I should do next—bring the women to the main party.

"Thomas, please come here," he called out to one of his officials. "I'd like to invite Vanessa and the other ladies to our party. What do you think?"

"Well, sir, I think they are busy already. Remember, they have a fashion show after they finish eating."

"Then see if the show is over. If so, they can join us. And bring Vanessa to sit beside me."

Thomas nodded and headed to the ladies' quarters. Before he reached the door to leave, the room went dark.

There was immediate silence from the men, followed by a roar of confused voices as everyone talked at once.

"What happened to the lights?"

"I can't see anything. What's happened?"

Mr. King spoke loudly and clearly. "Silence, everyone! If you will look out the patio doors, you'll see the whole street has lost electricity. There must be a total blackout. Please stay in your seats. I'll find a flashlight and figure out what is going on."

Fortunately, one of the waiters had picked up a lighted torch from the garden patio and gave it to Mr. King.

"This is excellent. Thank you. Please find more of these and set them in this room."

With the ability to see, King hurried to the door where he found Martin and asked what was going on.

"Sir, I wish I knew, but I'm sure going to find out. In fact, I was just heading off to take some lights to the ladies' quarters," Martin said.

"No, I'll do that. You go on and see if you can get the lights back on. Of all nights for this to happen!"

They went their separate ways. Without electricity, the elevators weren't working so King had to go up the stairs to reach the ladies' floor. The shadows and sounds echoed throughout the floor made the room hard to find. After opening and closing a few doors, he opened one that already had lights. There were a dozen lit candles around a chaise lounge draped with luscious purple silk sheets, and right in the middle of this beautiful scene was Vanessa and a man in a deep embrace.

"What is going on here, Vanessa?" King shouted.

"King, what are you doing here?" Vanessa jerked her head toward the door where he was standing. Her eyes were wide with a hint of panic as she hurriedly pulled her gown back onto her shoulders.

"Checking to make sure you're OK, which, obviously, you are," he said, his voice icy. He looked toward the man. "And you are?"

Jumping to his feet, the man started to put out his hand but then, realizing that wasn't such a good idea, brought it back. "Um, my name is Jack. Sir Jack Forrester and, um ... a friend of Vanessa's. I met her a few months ago during her shopping trip to England. I guess you don't care about any of that," he added with a stammer. His face flushed as he pulled on his shirt.

"Vanessa, you have three minutes to get your stuff together and get out of my store. I can't believe you would deceive me in such a public way. And to think I wanted you to be my wife, the mother of my children. I trusted you."

"Oh, King, I can explain!" Vanessa stumbled over to where King stood.

Pushing her arms away, he again told her to leave.

"By the way, all the electricity is gone from the store and I believe the street. Have fun finding your way out, but make sure you do."

Crying, she grabbed her shawl and ran from the room, as did Jack. King stood there in shock. He thought he was a great judge of character. He thought he had his life all set in perfect order. He thought he had found his queen who would rule with him forever.

All his hopes and dreams were dashed and his confidence in himself shattered. Collecting himself, he walked out of the room and finally found the ladies' banquet room. Fortunately, Martin was already there. Torch lights illuminated the rooms. The ladies were relieved to see him, especially when he said they were doing everything possible to get the lights back on.

"Right now, the best and safest thing for you to do is stay put," he said to the concerned ladies. "You have plenty of places to sit or lie down, and we still have plenty of food and drink to make your stay comfortable. If you want to leave this room and wait with your husband, just let me know."

Evie could tell none of the women wanted to leave their friends and the beautiful room so they stayed and continued to have a wonderful time. The fashion show had ended before the lights went out, so all the models, still in their beautiful fashions, came to the room and the safety of the torches. The guests were thrilled they didn't have to leave this once-in-a-lifetime party and continued to talk with each other. The models walked around and let the ladies touch and feel their exquisite fashions up close and, hopefully, increase their desire to purchase.

Evie had not been afraid when the lights went out but had been genuinely concerned for the guests. And then she was for herself and Uncle Martin. Could someone have caused the lights to go out? Fortunately, Margie had been there for the show, so she and Evie were able to sit together while waiting for light. Evie decided to look at the situation as a fun occasion so as not to worry—a giant spend-the-night party but with gorgeous fashions, delectable food, and plenty of cushiony sofas and chaise lounges to rest on.

When Mr. King came into the room, Evie felt like a knight in shining armor had come to rescue them. He did an amazing job calming everyone and dispersing their fears. She knew there was something incredibly special about that man. Here was one of the most important nights of his life, yet he took the time and energy to reassure the women. His actions calmed the whole room. The next few hours went well without anyone getting anxious or desperate with fear. The ladies rested and enjoyed the amenities that were provided for them.

The lights came back on after a ten-hour total blackout over Manhattan. The cause was a series of power failures occurring over several Northeastern states and parts of Canada. The blackout covered 80,000 miles and affected more than thirty million people. Despite the confusion, there were few cases of rioting, looting, or other crimes during the blackout. The next day, the newspapers called it, "The Great Blackout of 1965."

By dawn, everyone was ready to leave. And even though Mr. King thought the evening had been a total disaster, the word on the street and in the newspapers was that Mr. King outdid himself once again.

CHAPTER SEVEN

On Monday, Mr. King asked for his top officials to come to an early, emergency meeting. Once seated around the large conference table, Mr. King began.

"Gentlemen, I hired each one of you because I believed you had the character and the moral integrity to stand by me and help me grow King's into one of the finest stores in the world. I believe our banquets on Saturday showed the world what we are trying to achieve, and though I thought the evening might have been a failure, I now believe we had a great success. King's is at the top of the list of where to find the best quality and the finest assortment of items anyone in the world could wish for."

Everyone cheered, but King raised his hand to silence them.

"However, though I thought I had great insight in hiring and trusting people, I learned during the blackout my skills in this area might have been lacking."

He recounted his meeting with Vanessa. "So, she's gone, and I'm in a state of shock. Do any of you have suggestions for what I should do? If the public finds out the 'Queen' of King's has cheated on me, I'm afraid the women will lose their trust in me and King's. Vanessa was the leader for them in the world of fashion, with King's being the center hub. I'm at a loss as to how to deal with this PR disaster."

Silence fell on the room as the men took in this news, their faces showing shock. Some moved restlessly in their chairs, some took a sip of water, but no one said anything.

But then Thomas opened his notebook, picked up his pen, and spoke. "King, I've been thinking of some PR to suggest to you when the time was right. I believe the time has arrived. First, we don't say a thing about Vanessa being gone. Everyone in New York is still on a high from the weekend's glorious events. Tell the fashion department that Vanessa is on a much-needed vacation.

"Next, send out an announcement in the *New York Times* that King's is having a model competition. Every woman who is age eighteen to twenty-five is invited to apply. The contest could be held in what—two or three months? That would give us plenty of time to sort out the details and give our PR/Marketing department time to really build on this. The winner would be crowned, 'Queen of King's' and she would then represent our store in our newspaper, magazine, and store ads. What do you think?"

There was a murmur of excitement throughout the room. Many heads nodded.

"Thomas, I think you might have the answer," King said. "This is a great idea. Yes, get the ball rolling. And please, everyone, don't say a word about what happened between me and Vanessa. I don't need the embarrassment."

"You have our word, King," said one official, shaking King's hand in a show of solidarity.

"Please don't worry," another said. "Concentrate on keeping the momentum from the weekend's banquets going."

Thomas added, "King, keep the workers from tearing down the ladies' banquet room. That area is the perfect place for the contest to be held."

"Another perfect idea, Thomas. Thank you."

Evie and Margie arrived at the store while Mr. King was in his conference. Vanessa had asked Evie to help put the show merchandise back in the proper departments, and the Ford agency agreed Evie could help. Margie had hours of follow-through work from the banquets' design campaign. As they walked through the store, they could see hundreds of workmen taking down the elaborate décor from the main floor. Evie had no idea how long that would take but she was glad she was only working on the fashion clothing. First, she had to find Uncle Martin. She reached his office just as he was putting his coat on the hook behind the door.

"Good morning, little Evie." Martin said. "How are you today after this past wild weekend?"

"Hi, Uncle. The entire weekend was a spectacle and an emergency just waiting to happen when those lights went out. You did a great job bringing torches to our room. Margie and I sighed in relief when we saw you. And I'm doing great today, thank you, though still somewhat tired. Even my eyes are heavy from looking at those beautiful rooms."

"We were fortunate to have enough gas torch lights for both rooms."

"I do have something I need to talk to you about. On Saturday morning, Margie and I talked with a young woman about our age. I think she's homeless. I sent her up to the workers' area for food, but I also asked her to come back today and talk to you about a job. Is there anything you could find for her?"

"Well, let me see. About your age?" he asked.

"Yes, really sweet … and colored. Will that be a problem?"

"Um, well, we actually could use another helper in the kitchen. Give me her name, and I'll watch for her. Evie, that's really kind of you to help someone out."

"I'd want someone to do that for me if I was destitute," Evie said. "Her name is Anna. Thanks so much. Have a great day."

"You too, little Evie. You too."

The rest of the day was fun for Evie. Touching and being around fabulous couture was one of her favorite parts of being a model. She also liked the visual merchandising aspect of working on the sales floor, setting up showcase displays with the most sought-after styles, and wardrobing the mannequins in a way to grab the eye. She spotted Vanessa's head assistant several times and wondered if Vanessa had taken the day off.

"Janie, hi," Evie said. "Where's Vanessa today? I wanted to make sure I put the dresses back in the best places."

"Thank you so much for coming in today. I understand she went on a much-needed vacation, which is kind of weird because she was in England last month. But if I had her money, I'd go on a vacation whenever I could. You do whatever you think best with the dresses and fashions. You probably have a better sense of what works than anyone at the store."

"I do love being in this department. But now that you're here, I think I'll get some lunch. Want me to pick up anything for you?"

"Not a thing, but take your time. Looks like you've already put this area back in order."

After lunch, Evie could hear a buzz of excitement throughout the store and was on her way to find Margie when they met in the hall. Margie was out of breath.

"Guess what?" Margie asked. "King's is having a contest—a modeling contest in three months. In three months! The winner will be crowned 'Queen of King's' and will be the spokesperson and face for King's. Can you believe it? We just got the news in design, and the place is a madhouse. Every woman in the New York City area who is eighteen to twenty-five can enter. It's like Cinderella or something."

"I never heard of such a thing," Evie said. "Sounds a little like the Miss New York contest or as you said, Cinderella. Three months from now? Do you think I should apply?"

"Oh, Evie, of course you should. That's why I've chased you down. Because you *will* win!" Margie laughed.

"That's to be determined, but you help me find the perfect dress, and we'll see."

CHAPTER EIGHT

The store was nonstop busy over the next three months—so much so Evie could hardly keep up. Along with her assignments from the Ford agency, one of Vanessa's assistants asked her to help in the fashion areas as the contestants poured into the store looking for dresses, shoes, and jewelry.

At last, the day of the contest arrived.

Evie sat at her dressing table to finish her makeup. The contest would start soon. She kept her long blonde hair curled and pulled up on both sides with a gemstone clasp. Margie had helped her find *the* perfect dress. When she put it on, some of the women stared. The dress was that beautiful.

Gold, with an outer layer of transparent gold silk, the strapless bodice had straps of gold satin fabric crisscrossed and nestled into the slim waistline. Gemstones and sequins covered the dress and train. When Evie walked and turned, her whole dress sparkled. A single diamond solitaire necklace and matching earrings finished the look.

Yes. She swirled in front of the large mirror. *This dress is perfect.*

To keep the number of contestants to a reasonable number, the marketing department had held preliminary auditions. From hundreds of contestants, they narrowed the field to fifty ladies. These were the most beautiful women in the New York City area, and the press was having a field day.

Backstage, Evie was not nearly as nervous as the other contestants, who were pacing and talking excitedly with each other. She didn't think she had a chance when she saw the other women. They were all drop-dead gorgeous, as well as intelligent. Part of the contest was sharing what you thought America and New York, in particular, needed and how you could help with that problem. These women were articulate and brilliant. Many had attended college.

As each girl was called and walked down the runway, Evie heard the oohs and aahs from the crowd. It was like nothing she had ever witnessed. The answers the girls gave for what they thought should be done in America were as insightful and as intelligent as Evie thought they would be.

Well, I know I won't win this one, but I sure will have fun, plus I'll get the experience of a lifetime.

Evie heard her name. Confident from experience on a runway, head up, shoulders back, she allowed a smile to spread across her face.

The second the spotlight shone on her gold and sparkly dress, Evie almost couldn't walk with all the commotion from the audience. They even clapped as she began her walk. By the time she got back to the center stage in front of the judge's booth, she could still hear the crowd talking and exclaiming about her and her dress.

"Hello, Number Seven, how are you tonight?" asked the first judge. "Are you ready to discuss your subject?"

"Yes, I am, thank you. And I'm doing very ..." As she was about to finish her sentence, she spotted Mr. King. She didn't realize he would be one of the judges. He looked so stunning in a velvet tux with a satin lapel. He smiled at her, and when their eyes met, her knees began to tremble. She had a hard time concentrating on the judge's question.

"Yes, I'm doing well!" she answered. "My challenge to America and cities like New York is to focus on the poverty and the homeless population we have in our great country. Yes, we will always have the poor because of bad decisions and broken people. However, we must take care of the women and children affected by this poverty. We need housing for them, places for daycare, and job opportunities. My plan, though, is for the community to take care of this, not the government. When people think the government will take care of problems, they stop wanting to be involved. Our churches, synagogues, mosques, and corporations should reach out to those in their particular community and be a resource of help for these homeless."

"Thank you, Number Seven for your thoughtful answer."

Margie was waiting backstage, a big smile on her face. "Oh, Evie, you were just so, so ... perfect. If you don't win, then the judges are crazy."

"Margie, the judges are fine. All these women are spectacular. I really don't expect to win." She paused. "Listen. they're calling the numbers for the top ten."

As they waited in the wings, the girls could hear the numbers called out.

"Numbers 3, 47, 14, 26, 42, 31, 39, 19, 21, and 7. You are in our top ten. Those not in the top ten, thank you for entering the contest."

"You did it, you did it, you got in the next group!" Margie jumped up and down. "Go get ready to line up." She pushed an incredibly surprised Evie to the line of women who would walk out on the stage again.

Evie was still in shock when she stepped back on the stage with the other contestants. On either side of her were the most amazing women she'd ever met. She had started a friendship with many of them during the last few weeks and would be happy if any one of them won.

During this part of the judging, each contestant had to elaborate on her chosen project. Evie was ready when her turn came.

"Number Seven, could you explain a little more about your helping the poor and homeless project?"

"Yes, thank you. I'm thrilled to have the chance to share my concept. I envision a small building in the shape of a circle called Circle of Hope. Each pie-shaped section would house a different area of need for the homeless: One section for sleeping, one for eating, one for daycare, one for teaching a trade, and perhaps one for medical help.

"Each person who receives help would be responsible for giving back to the center, such as helping in the kitchen or the daycare. That way, the house wouldn't be charity but a place of hope. Grocery stores close by could donate bread and food, as could restaurants. Corporations could donate money, personnel, etc. These buildings could be constructed very simply so they could pop up in every needy part of the country. The homeless would have hope for their future and a place where they could receive food. Too many in our rich country are starving."

"Thank you for your answer," replied one of the judges.

After all the contestants had expanded on their answers, the judges asked for a short recess so they could add up their scores. The contestants were quiet as they sat in the backstage area, perhaps because they were trying to remember if they could have said more. Evie believed she could have. Thirty minutes later, they returned to the stage where they stood in line in front of the judge's table.

The main judge stood. "We have reached a decision. This has been most difficult because the beauty and the thoughtful answers of this group of women far surpassed anything we had even hoped to see. As you all know, each one of you was judged on your posture and confidence as you modeled as well as your ability to engage and answer difficult questions. You were also judged on how you responded in a large crowd. Without more delay, the winner of the King's Beauty and Modeling Contest is ... Evangeline Emerson!

Evangeline jerked her head from left to right as she tried to make sense of what the judge said. She still had a hard time processing the situation even as the other contestants crowded around her to hug and congratulate her.

Mr. King approached the microphone and smiled. "Miss Emerson, I can't tell you enough how thrilled I am personally that you won. You have been such an asset to this store in every capacity and to know you will continue here as 'The Queen of King's' brings all of us such delight. Congratulations!"

He continued when the applause subsided. "I have the privilege of placing this crown on your head." He handed her a beautiful bouquet of roses, then he leaned in and whispered in her ear, "You did great." With the orchestra playing a triumphant march, Evie took a final stroll down the runway amid tremendous applause. King's had its Queen on a day she would never forget.

CHAPTER NINE

A few weeks after the contest, Evie dropped in to see her uncle. As she approached his office, she could see him at his desk.

"Knock, knock. May I come in?" she asked.

"Evie, my dear, how good to see you today. What brings you to my part of the store?"

"I had some free time and wanted to know how Anna was doing," Evie said. "You were so kind to give her a job."

"Anna's doing great and told me she loves working in the kitchen—brings back memories of cooking with her grandmother down in Georgia. She shares an apartment with a sister and brother, so things are going fine for her." Martin grinned. "You sure was sweet to see that she needed help. Wish'n more people would do the same, I do. You know your Meemaw would often say, 'Wherever there is a human being, there is an opportunity for kindness.'"

"You're right about that. I'm thrilled you were able to find a place for her. By the way, when can you come by for dinner with Margie and me? I should have invited you before now, but we've been crazy busy."

"Oh, I'll come anytime. How about Wednesday night? Not too much going on during a weeknight, and I don't have to check the store after hours."

"That's perfect. Margie and I will check on our recipes and see what we can whip up. Come around seven? We'll have fun catching up."

"Will do, Evie. Thanks so much for the invitation and a chance to see how much little Princess has grown."

"Oh, you wouldn't believe how big she is and how spoiled. I sure love her and thank you again for giving her to me."

As Evie left the security office, she saw Mr. King on his way in.

"Hello, Evie. Nice to see you this morning. I need to talk with Martin about a few things, but would you wait for me? I'd like to talk to you."

"Sure, I'll wait outside."

As Evie waited, she could feel her palms getting moist and her heart pounding. *This is ridiculous. He's my boss— that's all. Why am I so nervous every time I see him? I really need to figure out how to distance myself from him.*

She could tell there was more to King than what was apparent because of all Uncle Martin had shared about him and what she had seen personally. He wasn't a player, a playboy, an Adonis, or a man after money and fame. He had mentioned he wanted to give back to the city that had embraced him when he first moved here.

As she waited for him, she contemplated how much had changed since winning the modeling contest. She greatly missed working for the Ford agency, but felt working at King's would give her résumé more depth. Her job now was much more flexible. Her new full-time duties included working with the fashion shows each week as well as modeling for them, writing articles about the store for newspapers, and representing the store while being interviewed for women's magazines, including *Vogue*, *Woman's Day*, and *Good Housekeeping* about all aspects of women's fashions. Yes, this new position was even better than she could have hoped for.

"Evie, thanks for waiting," King said. "Would you walk with me back to my office? We can talk on the way."

As they headed in that direction, King's fast pace, frequent smiles, and willingness to talk showed Evie he was in a particularly good mood. Thankfully, she was tall and able to keep up with his pace.

"I wanted to talk to you about some other ways you can be the face of King's. I would like for you, the marketing department, and me to meet tomorrow morning and work on ideas to bring important people into the store—authors, painters, inventors, etc. Each month could highlight a different person, and you would be the spokesperson for the advertisements, inviting everyone to King's for this wondrous event. What do think?"

"Great idea. I'll compile a list of potential people and begin contacting them. The problem might be matching schedules. I think this idea will be a great success for the store."

"Good! I'll set up the meeting for tomorrow morning in my office at nine." He glanced at his watch. Noon. "Would you care to eat lunch with me in the tearoom?"

"That would be nice, thank you," Evie's heart thumped in her chest so hard she was afraid he could hear it. How should she act? No way could she eat around him—she wouldn't be able to swallow a bite. Her legs were already beginning to shake.

Lunch was delightful. Mr. King had a way of bringing out the best in people, making you feel like you were the only one in the room. Evie shared stories of her life in boarding school, causing them both to laugh at the crazy stories she shared.

She was sad when he asked if she was finished and then stood to go.

"Thank you, Evie, for such a delightful lunch. I don't know when I've enjoyed one as much." He pulled out her chair and walked her to the elevator. "I'll see you tomorrow at nine. Until then."

As the elevator doors closed, King let out his breath. He hadn't realized he had barely taken a breath the whole time he had been with Evie. What was it about this young woman? Yes, she was extremely beautiful, but he'd been around beautiful women all his life. There was just something so pure, so kind, so real about her that he wanted to be in her company all the time.

Her winning the modeling contest was a miracle. She was younger—less experienced—than the other contestants. Of course, he had voted for her, but he had no way of knowing the other judges had too. In fact, she got almost every vote. Now he needed to figure out how to get to know her better, as well as how to be around her without losing his breath or his confidence.

He had been so hurt by Vanessa's deception he hadn't dated since she left. He was a broken man. But he also realized brokenness could be a good thing, which meant he was able to see himself and his life in a different light. He allowed himself time to think, meditate, and pray for the first time in a long while. He knew he was changing into a better man. Hopefully, Evie would think so too. Starting tomorrow he would get to know her better.

CHAPTER TEN

As Evie walked back to her office after lunch with King, she saw Margie. "Guess who I just ate lunch with."

"I guess Mr. Martin. Who else do you see but him and me?"

"How about Mr. King?"

Margie's mouth dropped open. "What?"

"I'll give you a full report this evening. I also saw Mr. Martin and invited him for dinner Wednesday night. Does that work?"

"Yes, sounds great but hearing what happened at lunch will sound better."

That night after eating dinner with Margie and filling her in with the details of her lunch with King, Evie climbed into bed and stared at the ceiling, thinking about him.

To Evie, he looked like a rock star or a famous movie star. He was tall with thick brown hair and blond highlights from the sun. He had a tan, and the way he wore his suit ... well, he had some amazing shoulders underneath his custom made Yves Saint Laurent suit.

Uncle Martin once shared that King was one of the most intelligent, down to earth, kindest, and most thoughtful men he had ever met.

After she started modeling for the store, she'd encountered Mr. King more often but at that time, he was in love with Vanessa. She never got the chance to talk to him one on one until after the great banquets. By then, Vanessa had left in disgrace, and Evie was focused on trying to help the fashion department get back on its feet. Mr. King had met with them many times, and each time she saw him, he knew her name and included her on all the decisions for that department.

Now she was Queen of King's. The thought made her smile and hug her pillow to her chest. Even Princess seemed happy as she snuggled up next to her before curling back into a ball. Evie would get to see King all the time now. He had even asked her to attend the management meetings. She would bring a notebook to jot down her ideas for the store.

The next day, she was at King's before nine. Uncle Martin was at the front door to let management in early.

"Martin, it's so good to see you this fine morning. Margie and I can't wait to see you tomorrow night for dinner. We have a great meal planned with your favorites, including fried chicken and mashed potatoes, with peach cobbler and vanilla ice cream for dessert. How does that sound?"

"I'm looking forward to the dinner too, Evie. In fact, I can hardly wait to have some home cooking, especially with so many of my favorites. That's too nice of you and Margie. I see you're going to the management meeting at Mr. King's office."

"Yes, and to tell you the truth, I can hardly wait. I have so many ideas."

"I think you're the first one here. Go on up. You have time to get some coffee. See you later."

Evie gave him a quick hug and walked to the elevator. In the waiting area outside Mr. King's office, she found steaming coffee, with containers of cream and sugar. *Nothing is better than "coffee-milk"*—a reminder of boarding school and how the girls would add so much cream and sugar to their coffee they called it coffee-milk. The tradition stuck with her. Mr. King joined her as she added the cream.

"Good morning, Evie." Mr. King greeted her as he walked to the coffee station. "I see you like your coffee the way I do."

Evie almost dropped her mug in surprise that he was already there. "Yes, I do like lots of cream in my coffee. We called it coffee-milk at boarding school."

"Sounds like a perfect adjective to describe it. Ready to go on into my office? We can talk and enjoy our coffee while waiting for the others to join us."

His office was just what Evie had imagined—mahogany furniture, lush oriental carpet, beautiful old paintings on two of the paneled walls, and a large bookshelf full of leather-bound books. The large sofa opposite his massive desk, as well as club chairs, a love seat, and a dozen chairs around a table offered plenty of seating. It was a huge room but the sun shining through a large window behind his desk made the entire area warm and welcoming.

"I have to ask ... these landscape paintings are extraordinary. Who are the artists?"

"You have a good eye. The painting with the people walking on the beach is one of my favorites. John Singer Sargent painted *The Oyster Gatherers of Cancale* in 1878.

"But this larger painting, *Italian Landscape with Bridge and Tower* by J. M. W. Turner, is older—1827. He's one of the greatest landscape artists of all time and perhaps the most renowned British artist ever. He was able to capture the effects of color and light, which made him famous as "the painter of light," along with his application of an imaginative approach to landscape art. In his later years, his compositions became more fluid with mere suggestion of movement. These abstractions are considered ahead of his time and a forerunner to the artistic movement Impressionism, which Claude Monet perfected. I'm sure you've seen some of Monet's Water Lily paintings?"

"Oh yes! I saw one on the wall in the men's banquet room. It's beautiful."

"I had that painting installed for the banquet. I think Monet is my favorite artist of all time. Evie, art, artists, and authors are some of my great loves. Now, take this chair." He guided her to the club chair next to his desk."

She thanked him and took a seat. "I love your office, Mr. King. The colors and décor are exceptional."

"Please call me King. And thank you. I had the office redecorated after Venessa left and knowing you like the change makes it even better." He smiled and shot her a look that went right through her. As she took a sip of her coffee, she didn't think she would be able to swallow.

As the rest of the team arrived, Evie grew quiet, enjoying her coffee and the conversation of men who cared for and respected each other, as well as Mr. King and his store. She could already tell she would love being a part of this inner circle.

King motioned toward the conference table. "Shall we begin the meeting?"

"Evie, sit here next to me so, if I say anything wrong, you can kick me under the table."

"Oh, sir, I don't think that will ever be necessary," she said amidst a chorus of laughter. Her face heated.

"As you all know, this is Evangeline, aka Evie, who was recently crowned Queen of King's. I believe you will all agree with me she'll be a tremendous addition to every aspect of King's. We welcome you, Evie, to our team."

Everyone clapped, making Evie feel included. She was also relieved because a group of important businessmen could have tried to make her, as a woman, feel inadequate and not important. She knew, because King welcomed her so warmly, the other men would follow suit.

Throughout the morning's meeting, she remained quiet, mainly to make sure she could listen and learn from these men. She had her notebook open and took notes. When the meeting was over, King asked her to stay.

"Tell me, Evie, what do you think of our little group of merry men? I noticed you taking notes. Would you allow me to see your notebook?"

Evie handed the notebook over with some trepidation, not knowing what he would say.

"Your notes are excellent. You captured our conversation exactly. Very good job, indeed. From now on, if you don't mind, I'd like to see what you have written after each meeting, so I won't forget a thing."

"I'd be happy to do that. Glad I'm not kicked out of the group so soon."

King looked her straight in her eyes. "Don't ever worry about that. You're part of the team."

Evie almost fainted.

CHAPTER ELEVEN

The next few months were a whirlwind for Evie, as well as King's. Spring tourists from all over the world made the store one of their top destinations to visit along with the Statue of Liberty and the Empire State Building. Sales were through the roof and the staff had a hard time keeping the shelves filled. King and his buying group traveled more to find the perfect items customers were coming to expect to find at King's. These months were a fun and exhilarating time to be a part of this fast-moving tide of retail.

King consulted her on many decisions—if the décor of the store should be changed; should the store have more fashion shows, etc.

Evie sensed something was going on between them. She didn't know if he felt the same way, even though he acted as if he cared for her too. Perhaps King was taking his time, not wanting to make the same mistake he made with Vanessa. Evie was fine with things coming along slowly. She remembered the times when a group of her friends from fashion school would meet up with guys from other schools. She soon learned becoming friends was always the best way to begin any relationship. Some of the guys wanted more but she was determined not to get involved in a relationship at that point in her life. Her heart opened with joy when she saw King, and when she wasn't with him, she counted the hours until she would see him again. That was enough for now.

One afternoon, as Evie stepped into King's office, she found him and Martin almost whispering.

"Should I come back another time?"

"No, Evie, you need to hear this. Martin has just given me some startling news. It appears a coup is in the process of forming."

"Say that again?"

"The idea is hard even to imagine, must less repeat, but while Martin stood by the main door this afternoon, two men, whom he had never seen, walked in and began to survey the first floor. They then walked to an alcove and talked in hushed tones. Fortunately, Martin had the instinct not to address them but got close enough to hear their words. They mentioned that, soon, they would own King's. That if their plan of "putting King in the ground," along with buying all the remaining stock, succeeded, they would then own this store."

Kill King? No! Evie sank onto the sofa. "How can they be thinking about killing you? We live in America!"

"It happens more often than you would realize." King's voice shook with anger. "The Mafia is alive and well, and my guess is, they want this store for laundering money, as well as bringing in a great number of drugs. I think the threat is real, so I have asked the FBI to come in this afternoon. Nobody, absolutely nobody can take what I've built."

"Everything will turn out OK," Martin said. "The FBI will get these men. I'm thrilled you took my advice and installed those surveillance cameras. The sixties are heading toward the future. Now we can show the footage to the FBI, and hopefully, they can identify the men."

"I'd like to be in the meeting with the FBI, and I believe your secretary should be there also," Evie said.

King nodded. "I agree. You and Mrs. Howard are to be in on the meeting. The only reason I put in those cameras was to make my store look ahead of the times. Thank goodness we have them."

As Evie and Martin left his office until the meeting with the FBI, Evie asked Martin to walk her back to her office.

"Martin, do you think these men are part of the group searching for us? I'm so afraid."

"Evie, I don't think so in this case. This seems like a New York City mafia at work. Let's not get too worried until we see what the FBI has to say."

Although distraught, Evie was thrilled she would be in the meeting with the FBI as they watched the videos. Fortunately, the FBI recognized the men instantly because they were so entrenched in the Mafia that the FBI had boxes of files on them. However, there wasn't anything they could do. The men had only talked about what they wanted to do. Nothing against the law had occurred. But at least the authorities knew who they were, could keep watch on them, and could let them know their plot had been discovered.

King and Martin kept the incident quiet to avoid fear in their staff or the public. But King and the entire security force worked more diligently in case anyone else tried to hurt King or sabotage his store. The situation also caused Martin to be more alert in case anyone was snooping around looking for him or Evie.

"Mr. King, I'm sure thankful we got these men before they could carry out their plans," Martin said a few days later. "But are you aware of what's happening in the South these days?"

"I've heard of some protests or riots. Should we be concerned this far away?"

"Remember the riot in Harlem a couple of years ago? An off-duty police officer shot and killed that fifteen-year-old colored boy in Manhattan. Things really got bad."

"I remember the incident somewhat, but the upheaval ended quickly. So?"

"Then there was the Watts Riot, called the Watts Rebellion, a couple of years ago in Los Angeles with the colored people protesting. Turned into six days of burning and rioting and thirty-four people died. They are mighty frustrated with the poverty and lack of jobs.

"All the white people have moved out of the cities, leaving nothing for those who can't move out. The reason I'm bringing this up now is we might have the Mafia breathing down our necks, Mr. King, but I'm worried about more riots. The Ku Klux Klan is alive and active down South and causing a lot of misery for my people. Remember "Bloody Sunday?""

King nodded.

"All those people wanted to do was march in peace to the Edmund Pettus Bridge outside Selma. They were marching fifty-four miles from Selma to Montgomery, the state capital of Alabama. That's down near my people. They were ordered to disperse and then moments later, the police assaulted them with tear gas, bullwhips, and billy clubs.

"Well, sir, I'm afraid more problems like these could happen again and right here in New York. I want you to know I'm keeping my ears and eyes open in case anyone tries to do the same here. You never know who might want to start working here just because they want to start something."

King thought this over. "I'm indebted to you for thinking ahead. I've heard bits and pieces of the unrest you've mentioned. My head is so into fashion and buying I don't pay much attention to what's going on in the world. So, please keep on the alert! If you see anyone, of any color, trying to start something in our part of the world, you let me know."

Martin smiled. "Yes, sir, I sure will. I'm not letting anything hurt you, Evie, or your store and its people."

Early one fall day, King gave himself a break from paper work. He gazed toward the Turner landscape painting but his thoughts were on Evie. After learning someone wanted to kill him, he started contemplating his future and how he wanted to spend the rest of his life. And that life, he decided, included Evie. She had a calming effect on him. Nothing rattled her, and she always had a smile on her face. He'd never known anyone who was as kind and compassionate. She was a rare treasure. He hoped she thought as highly of him.

Vanessa had been gone almost a year. The store was doing better than ever, and King knew the time had come to approach Evie personally. He wanted to ask her out on a real date, but how? Every time he saw her, his heart stopped, and he couldn't speak. She probably didn't even consider him date worthy. He decided, after their staff meeting the next morning, he would ask her out for dinner. Everyone must eat, so they might as well eat together. *If I can talk with dignitaries and royalty across the world, I can certainly ask one woman to go on a date.*

The next morning, King paced his office. In mid-stride, he ran his finger around his damp collar. He really must keep an extra shirt in his office. Too late today. He had to calm down before Evie came to the staff meeting. Fortunately, when he saw her come through the door, her irresistible smile and warm "hello" helped him relax.

"Evie," King said after the meeting, "I wonder if you would like to get a bite to eat tonight? I mean, we could continue to discuss … stuff."

Evie smiled. "That would be great. What time were you thinking?"

"Time? Oh yes, time! How about seven? I could pick you up at your apartment, and we could go to the pub near you I've heard so much about."

"That sounds perfect." Evie smiled.

Evie was over the top excited. King had finally asked her out. She could barely walk down the hallway without wanting to jump or dance. What would she wear? She needed to go shopping right away and where better than in King's Ladies' Wear Department? She browsed until she found a soft blue cashmere sweater and light weight black wool pants.

At seven sharp, there was a knock on the door. Evie asked Margie to open the door, which she had been told was the proper way. When the door opened, Princess tried to escape.

"Oh, no, you don't," Margie said as she grabbed the cat. "You don't get to go on their date and get cat hair all over their clothes. You and I get to stay home."

Evie and King both laughed watching Margie hold on to the cat. But it helped ease Evie's first date jitters.

"OK, you kids have fun, and don't stay out too late," Evie rolled her eyes at Margie's quip as she and King stepped out the door.

"Since the pub is close by, I thought we'd walk," King said as they waited for the elevator. "I hope that's all right with you. By the way, you look great tonight." *Just like an angel.*

"I'd love to walk and thank you. You look good yourself—straight out of *GQ*." She thought he looked very handsome in a black turtleneck sweater and black pants.

The pub had become famous in the last year because of some of New York's famous people eating there. Somewhat like Studio 54, only less formal and no drugs. At least not yet. The pub was also famous for cheeseburgers and Reuben sandwiches. King and Evie found a cozy table in a corner where they could talk privately.

"What would you like to eat? I know models usually don't eat much, but I hope you will enjoy something tonight."

"Actually, I do eat. I'm just incredibly lucky to have a high metabolism, so I can eat almost anything. I also don't agree with models who are super thin. I know skinny is 'the look,' but some of these girls faint all the time. Tonight, I'm going with the pub's famous cheeseburger and a Coke. And if you order fries, may I have some?

King laughed, put down his menu, and looked at Evie. "I think I'm going to order the exact same thing."

King dreaded awkward moments, but after he placed their order, they fell into a natural rhythm of talking, listening, and sharing their lives. Long after the last French fry was eaten, they decided to stay on and ordered coffee.

Evie set down her cup. "King, this is so nice. Thank you for asking me out. I've wanted to know more about you."

"You have? I'm thrilled." King lowered his voice and moved closer to Evie, taking one of her hands in his. "I've wanted to ask you out for some time now but wasn't sure if you would want to. I'd like to see more of you. That is, more of you away from the store. Would you like to walk over to Central Park?"

"I'd love that."

King helped Evie from her chair, took her hand, and led her out of the pub toward the park. Just holding her hand and walking this close to her gave King a sensation he'd never had with any other woman—a revelation he could feel this deeply about another woman after Vanessa.

After walking through part of the park, they settled down on a bench, still talking and sharing bits and pieces of their lives. Soon, King looked at his watch. "Do you know what time it is? Midnight! I sure hope you don't disappear like Cinderella, but I need to take you home before Margie, Martin, or anyone else starts hunting for me."

"I can't believe we've talked for so long, but I've never enjoyed an evening as much."

Evie's apartment was close, and soon they were at her door. King took both of her hands in his and looked at her. "I want to kiss you goodnight more than I can say, but I'm not going to do that. You are such a special lady I want to take our time getting to know, really know, each other." King leaned down and kissed her lightly on her forehead. "Promise me you'll go out with me again."

Evie looked up at him with a sweet smile. "I promise."

The following weeks went by at the speed of light. No matter what King and Evie did, they loved spending time together, going to movies, dinner dates, or walking through the city they both loved. One of their favorite activities was to ride in his convertible throughout the countryside.

On one beautiful day, King called Evie's office phone.

"Evie, let's stop whatever we're doing and take a ride to the country with the top down. Can you get away?"

"You read my mind. I'm at a stopping point, so I can leave whenever you say."

"Great, let me pick you up at your office. We'll stop by Bennie's Deli for a picnic lunch. How does that sound?"

"Like heaven."

Ten minutes later, King stood at her office door, looking like a kid who was playing hooky from school. They walked together to his car, put the top down, stopped for the food, and were on the road.

As Evie started to wrap her scarf around her head the wind kept tearing it off.

She started to laugh which made King laugh. He pulled over to the side of the road so she could fix it, but neither could stop laughing.

The place they found for the picnic was perfect—a pond and plenty of soft grass made sitting on the quilt comfortable and beautiful.

"What a great idea to pick up sandwiches at Bennie's," said Evie. "I don't know when I've had a better lunch."

"I agree. I wish we could stay all day, but I have a board meeting tonight. Maybe one day we can have time together without having to race back to work.

"I do have an idea I wanted to ask you about, Evie. I know we've just started seeing each other these last few weeks, but I'd like to entertain again at my home. I know we both love to eat great food, and I would like for you to meet some of my friends away from work. Would you like to help Mrs. B, my housekeeper, with a meal and be hostess to a dinner party?

"I would love that. You know I love to cook, and I've been wanting to meet your Mrs. B. You've been to my apartment, but I haven't been able to see your home yet. Let's set a date and do it."

King checked his pocket calendar then said, "What about June 15? Gives us a couple of weeks to plan."

"Sounds great. Let me check my calendar when I get home, but I'm looking forward to cooking at your house for sure. And honored to be your hostess. I can't wait to get with Mrs. B and plan the menu."

One of King's favorite places to be was Evie and Margie's apartment—so warm and comfortable. He'd come by a few times after work and enjoyed one of her home-cooked meals. And what a cook she was. Evie could cook anything. And thankfully, Princess took to him right away. She jumped in his lap the first time he visited and never wavered from her devotion.

King and Evie never lacked something to talk about, and yet they were comfortable in silence too. They would talk about every subject imaginable: politics, fashion, goals, the future, and their faith. They agreed on most subjects, and on the ones they didn't, they agreed to disagree.

King felt he could talk to Evie about other, more deeply felt things—his feelings, his passions, his sad childhood, his goals for the store, and his desire to give back to others. She would listen and never criticize anything he said. He even shared his worst moment.

"Although Vanessa broke my heart, I'm thankful I found out who she really was. When she left, I was devastated to the point I thought my life was over. But when I hit bottom, I saw the truth. I decided then and there to change my ways and to become the man I admired in others. Character does matter, and I want to be honorable the rest of my life. I've also come back to my faith in God. I'll never put Him on a back burner again."

"I saw the change in you," Evie said. "That's what drew me to you. You have an authenticity that few people possess. I'm so glad we've been able to get to know each other. I feel I can share everything with you too, especially my childhood."

Evie shared that her parents had died when she was a little girl, and her grandmother believed she should leave home. Martin, a family friend, brought her to New York and supervised her inheritance, her education, and her safety. "I owe Martin so much. He's done everything for me."

One night after work, Evie and Margie had a simple dinner of vegetable soup and salad. They'd been so busy a free night was a rarity.

"Evie, isn't this nice to be home, relaxing just the two of us? I don't remember when we were home this early. I do love work, but I also love being home. And I think Princess misses us."

Evie sat back in her chair, drinking iced tea, and smiling at her best friend loving on Princess in her lap. The cat stretched and then curled up in a tight ball.

"Yes, I love being home too. We finally have time to sit, talk, and be together. We also have time to catch up on laundry and cleaning."

"I know, I know. How do mothers get everything done and take care of a baby too? I can barely take care of myself."

"Isn't that the truth? And now that I'm seeing King so much, there isn't as much time to keep up with everything. I never thought I'd be happy when he has a board meeting like tonight. If he could have one a week …"

"Oh Evie, you know you wish you could be with him every night! Which reminds me. I want to know all the latest juicy details of how you two are doing. Is your relationship getting serious?"

"Have I told you yet he asked me to be his hostess for a dinner party?"

"Yes, which is why I think this relationship is getting serious. Anything other than you cooking?"

"Oh, Margie, I can't believe I forgot to tell you we're going out of the city tomorrow to Connecticut. Only for the day, but we'll have more time than the few lunches or walks we try to catch during the workday. And you know, he still hasn't kissed me. Maybe this will be the time."

"I love getting out of the city. Tell me all about where you're going."

"The Bee and Thistle Inn. The pamphlet says the Inn is nestled on five glorious acres bordering the Lieutenant River. The Inn boasts about their delectable food, beautiful rooms, and lots of places to walk. We're going up for the day with a picnic and then an early dinner in their famous dining room before we head back to the city. Margie, I can't wait to have a full, uninterrupted day with King."

"The day sounds just heavenly, and I wish I could be a fly on the wall. Let's get the apartment cleaned up, and I'll help you pick your outfit for tomorrow."

King already had the top down on his convertible when he picked up Evie at ten o'clock sharp.

"Evie, I'm so excited about our trip today." King said as he opened the door and helped her into the car. "I've got lots planned for us and I sure hope you like everything."

"Don't worry—just being with you is all I need," Evie said as she gave him one of her beautiful smiles.

The weather was perfect, and the drive in an open car made them feel free with the sun and the wind on their faces. Shortly before they arrived at the Inn, they stopped at a small road-side vegetable shed where he purchased some homegrown tomatoes, corn, and peaches.

"I love fresh summer vegetables, King! These will be great for our dinner party in a few days. I'll make a peach cobbler."

Pulling up to the front entrance of the Inn, they saw a horse and carriage tethered to a post nearby.

"I think that's our next ride," King said to Evie. "I requested a carriage along with a picnic lunch. I hope you're ok with that?"

"Are you kidding? A carriage ride is the best idea I've heard in a long time."

The owner of the Inn came out, introduced himself, and walked with them to the carriage. He gave King a map of the property and pointed out some of the best picnic spots. Tipping his hat, he said, "Have a great time!"

When he returned inside the Inn, Evie looked at the horse, the carriage, and then at King. "Where is the driver?"

"I'm the driver! How hard could it be? I see the picnic basket, blanket, and pillows are all here."

King took her hand and helped her up to the high seat. Then he opened the map, chose a beautiful spot, picked up the reins and said to the horse, "Go."

The horse just stood there, his tail flicking off flies.

King tried again to get him to go. This time he picked up the reins, swatted them on the horses back, and said 'giddy up.' All the horse did was look back at them with disdain and then move his head back to the forward position.

Evie was doing all she could not to laugh but finally lost control. Mortified, King looked at her but then joined her laughter until both had to wipe tears from their eyes.

"Maybe I could get out and lead him?"

"You stay put. This will be a romantic drive if it kills me!" King laughed along with Evie.

Finally, the horse started walking, but then King couldn't figure out the map. Were they heading north or south? As he worked on smoothing out the folded map, the breeze kept flicking the paper in his face. Fortunately, the horse had done this before and led them right to the correct spot, put his head down, and started eating the grass.

"Well, I'll be. He knew where we were going all along. Come on, Evie, I'll help you down. Let's set the quilt and basket by that beautiful oak tree."

After setting up the quilt and blankets, they feasted on roast chicken, cole slaw, potato salad, yeast rolls and butter, iced tea, and warm apple crisp.

King leaned against the large pillow he'd positioned by the tree trunk and Evie sat close to him, his hand on hers. For a moment, the only sounds they could hear were the birds singing and the soft lap of the lake.

"King, this lake is much bigger than the pond where we had our first picnic, but I think that pond is my favorite place. What do you think?"

Smiling King replied, "I know what you mean. I loved the little pond and sharing a lunch with you. I'm glad we've continued to get away whenever we can. I also know I've never felt such peace and contentment as I do right now."

King gently pulled her close so he could see her face. He took a loose curl of hair and placed it behind her ear.

"Evie, no one has ever made me as happy or as alive as you do. I hope we can always be together. You are truly a special lady in my life." King leaned in and gave her their first kiss.

Evie answered with a kiss of her own.

The next few days flew by. King made a point of staying out from under foot as Evie and Mrs. B created a menu and decorated King's dining room with chargers to hold the antique china along with a lovely flower centerpiece. The large mahogany table seated twelve, so they invited five couples, including some Evie had not had a chance to meet. Seeing Evie talking and circulating among his friends thrilled King. She was a natural, and the dinner couldn't have gone better. He hoped one day she would call this her home.

Soon, everyone at the store and throughout the city knew they were an item. King knew he couldn't live another day without knowing she was his for always. He asked Evie to meet him on the first floor after the store closed. He dimmed the lights and placed dozens of candles on the fine jewelry glass countertops.

"King? Are you here?"

When she entered the department, King, holding a large bouquet of red roses, approached her, and got down on one knee. "Evie, I know we haven't known each other for very long, but would you do me the great honor of becoming my wife?"

His heart thudded double time until he saw joy fill her beautiful eyes.

Evie looked down at him and said, "Yes, oh, yes, I will marry you!"

King stood, laid the roses aside, and then kissed her, holding her tight.

"I'm so surprised. When did you decide to do this?" Evie laughed. "I've been with you all week and you never said a thing about this."

"I don't want to spend another day without you by my side, day or night. Come look at the rings and pick the one you want. Price is no object."

Evie looked at the beautiful and sparkling assortment of rings. Pear-shaped, emerald, princess—each one was perfect.

"I think I would rather have you pick the one you love best," she said. "Then I will know I'm wearing your heart's desire."

CHAPTER TWELVE

"Yes! Being your maid of honor is the greatest honor you could give me," Margie told Evie. "And to see you so happy literally makes me want to cry tears of joy. We've known each other almost all our lives and to know you have found such a great guy—well, I can't ask for anything else. When you told me King asked to see you after the store closed, I had a feeling tonight would be the night you'd get engaged. I'm glad I stayed up late. Did he take you out for a special dinner?

Margie and Evie were sitting in their apartment, drinking tea, and staring at her gorgeous diamond ring. Margie had about come unglued when Evie came home from her date with King, hand raised so the ring would grab her attention right away.

"Yes, he had planned the whole evening. Oh, Margie, I wish you could have been there. He had candles on all the glass jewelry counters, got down on one knee, and asked if I'd be his wife! And he looked amazing. Had on a beautiful new suit with a handkerchief in the top pocket and the biggest smile. I could choose any ring I wanted, but I asked him to pick out the ring he wanted me to have. Just look at it," Evie said as she showed off her new engagement ring in all directions. "After we picked out the ring, we took a taxi to the little pub where we had our first date, which was perfect because I still wore my business suit. We ordered the same thing as we had at our first date, and talked and laughed and started making wedding plans."

As they sat and talked about the wedding plans, Evie asked Margie a question that had been bothering her.

"I'm over the moon with King and can hardly wait until we're husband and wife, but I'm starting to get nervous. What if I don't make King happy? What if I'm not a good wife?"

Margie looked Evie in the eyes and took both her hands. "There isn't a single thing for you to worry about. What makes a great marriage is when both people are truly in love, truly like each other, and are healthy with their emotions. Being a great wife is when you wake up each morning asking yourself, 'What can I do for him today?' A great marriage is being unselfish, giving, and most of all, kind. Evie, you *are* that type of person, and so is King. Just enjoy every aspect of this wedding, for I know you will be blessed with a wonderful marriage."

The next morning, Saturday, King shared a late brunch with Evie and Margie. Margie almost knocked him over when she hugged him, telling him how wonderful he was to her Evie and how beautiful the ring was.

"Well, I'm thrilled we have your stamp of approval." King smiled. "And that you don't mind me taking her away as my wife."

"I'm so happy I think I'll just cry some more." Instead, Margie stuffed another bite of pancakes in her mouth.

Evie had created a beautiful brunch—fresh-squeezed orange juice, homemade buttermilk pancakes, bacon, grilled grapefruit halves, and, of course, coffee.

Princess jumped into King's lap. "Well, I guess I have her approval too. I think she'll like her new home. I'm so glad she likes me."

"How could anyone not like you, King?" replied Evie.

"Evie, this is all so delicious. How could any man be so lucky?" King asked.

Evie gave him a kiss on his cheek while filling up his coffee mug.

"I also want to show you girls what's on page one of the society section."

As King opened the newspaper, Evie and Margie gasped. There in black and white was a photo of King and Evie with a headline, "The King and Queen are engaged!"

The newly engaged couple knew their news would put the gossip columns and newspapers in a tailspin, but they weren't expecting a front page so quickly.

"The coverage is not just the *New York Times*," King added. "All the newspapers have devoted space for this. Honey, I guess you better get ready for a lot of flashbulbs going off."

"But how did the news spread so fast? We just got engaged last night."

"When the owner of a large store asks for candlelight and privacy in the jewelry department, I'm sure someone blabbed the news. I'd rather have the news get out now. We need to set the date and, hopefully, keep those reporters away from us for a while."

Evie thought for a moment. "I have the date! Let's get married around Valentine's Day. Nothing says love more than a wedding. What do you think? King? Margie?"

"I actually love the idea," King said. "I was thinking of a small ceremony, but now I think we should have a larger one. The publicity would be great for the store—do you mind, Evie, that I think like that?—there are too many people we need to invite. What do you think?"

Apparently, Margie decided it was time to put her two cents into the conversation. "Yes, you have to have a huge wedding. Too many people will want to attend. And, of course, it's good for the store!"

Evie started to laugh. "I agree with both of you. A large wedding it is. Margie, hand me my calendar, please."

The calendar revealed Valentine's Day fell on a Tuesday in 1967, so they chose Saturday, February 11 for the wedding.

"Looks like we've got a lot of work to do between now and then," Evie said. "Margie, I hope I don't work you too hard. We'll need a bridal consultant. I believe I'll ask Sara. I've worked with her in fashion shows, and she's done many of the weddings in New York. What do you think?"

"Sara will be perfect. She knows you and can help with many of the decisions," Margie said. "The next big step will be choosing the church and then the reception venue."

King had been quiet, enjoying listening to the two friends excitedly making plans. "Well, ladies, I will leave you two to it. I know I'm not needed until I say, 'I do.' Have fun, and Evie, get the wedding of your dreams. You'll never have another, so remember, price is not an object. I want my one and only Evie to be totally happy."

"Oh, King, I couldn't be happier! But I have the funds to pay for the wedding. Remember, the tradition is for the bride's family to pay for the wedding, and I still have my inheritance from my father's parents."

"That may be tradition, but I'm your only family now. I will pay for the wedding—my gift to you—and you save your inheritance."

With that, he gave her a kiss and left the apartment.

When Evie woke early on Monday morning, she still felt like she was living a dream. As the sunshine streamed through her curtains, her heart warmed at the thought she was engaged and planning a wedding. She looked at her hand where the diamond King had chosen sparkled in the daylight. She had never felt more loved.

Evie quickly got dressed and rushed to the store for her meeting with Sara. They had a tremendous number of decisions to make.

"Evie, it's Sara. May I come in?"

"Sara, you're right on time. Thank you for making time for me this morning. I need to be honest. I don't even know where to start. I've picked a date but that's all."

"No, you've picked a great guy first!" Sara laughed. "OK, the date you told me is Saturday, February 11, and the theme will be a Valentine's wedding. Correct?"

"Yes. I've also chosen the church, which I hope will be available. St. Patrick's Cathedral is the most beautiful church I've ever seen—I went there yesterday for services. Neither King nor I are Catholic but we both believe in God as our Lord. What do you think?"

"Perfect choice, Evie. Did you know St. Patrick's is the largest decorated Neo-Gothic-style Catholic cathedral in North America? And large enough to hold all your guests. The stained-glass windows of blues and reds will create the most beautiful atmosphere for your wedding. I'll call them right now."

"Thanks. I also love its location in Midtown on 5th Avenue—convenient for most everyone, plus, near where I hope we can have the reception."

"Where?"

"The Plaza! I can't think of any other place as beautiful or large enough for the reception. Can you call them also, and let's cross our fingers they aren't booked?"

Fortunately, both venues were available for Evie and King's wedding.

As Sara hung up the phone with the great news, Margie came into Evie's office.

"Hey, you two, how's the wedding planning going?"

"Guess what, Margie. We've just learned both my chosen venues are available—the beautiful St. Patrick's Cathedral and The Plaza."

"I should hope so. After all, the king and queen should have what they want. Now, what's next for us to do?"

"I need to work more on the guest list before we decide on the invitation paper and font. Sara will contact us in a few days about musicians and food for the reception. We need to pick out the bridesmaids' dresses and my dress and ... Do you think we can possibly be ready in time?"

"That's enough worrying. As Scarlett would say, 'Tomorrow is another day.'"

King came into Evie's office late one evening. "I thought I'd catch you here. Can we go out for dinner? You can tell me how the plans are going."

"I would love to have dinner with you, sweetheart. I'm starving. The plans are going well. Thank you for giving me this enchanting wedding. But I need to ask you—who will stand up for you as best man? I thought I would have multiple bridesmaids, but now I think I'll only have Margie. She's like my sister. I'd ask Sara but she'll behind the scenes making sure everything goes all right that night."

"That's funny. I was thinking the same thing. Thomas has been a friend longer than he's been an employee. So, keep it at one each?

"Yes, that sounds perfect. Even though the wedding will be large, having only our two best friends to stand up for us makes the ceremony much more intimate. Before I forget, there is one thing I want you to do. Will you plan where our wedding night will be, as well as choose the honeymoon location? I know we've talked about Europe, but really, I don't care where we go as long as I'm with you."

"You read my mind. I've already started planning both. All you will have to do is pack, and I'll give ideas to Margie and Sara to help you buy clothes for both. Now, let's get something to eat."

While Evie and Sara worked on the wedding plans, Margie came up with some great design and marketing ideas for the store.

"Evie and Sara, tell me what you think about this idea. Why not ask the design team to decorate the store with a Valentine wedding theme? We could hang giant hearts and baby's breaths throughout the store. Perhaps fill tubs and vases with red roses and place them strategically on counters and by the marble steps going up to the second floor. We can have crystal bowls full of chocolates on every table and counter in the jewelry and ladies' couture section. One more suggestion. Perhaps the Tea Room could serve complimentary champagne and heart-shaped sugar cookies with each meal until the day of the wedding."

Evie and Sara looked at each other with large smiles.

"Margie, those are perfect ideas! Yes, let's do them. Since our wedding date announcement, the store has never been busier. Your ideas will be the icing on the cake."

One late afternoon, Evie and Margie stopped on the staircase and saw with fresh eyes the beauty of King's and the decorations.

"You know, Margie, one would think I'd be tired of all this wedding planning and seeing the decorations, but the reverse is true. I don't know when I've been happier or enjoyed a process as much." Evie turned and looked at Margie. "And that's thanks to all you and Sara have done. Thank you, dear friend!"

"You're welcome. I agree with you. This has been a great experience for me too."

One decision Evie needed to make was who would give her away. She wanted Uncle Martin, of course, but would he agree? She feared he would say no. Evie called him on the phone and set a time they could visit privately in her apartment.

Since Margie was out, Evie gave Uncle Martin a giant hug.

"I'm so glad we could get together." Evie said.

"Me too, little Evie, me too. Your life is extra busy right now. Excited about the big day?"

"More than I can express. Come sit down. I have something I want to ask you."

Uncle Martin sank onto the sofa with a sigh. "I'm glad to get off my feet."

Evie had already made coffee, and some cookies were on the coffee table. She filled a cup for each of them.

"Thanks, Evie. Now, what did you want to talk about?"

Evie took a deep breath. "I wanted to ask you to please walk me down the aisle."

Uncle Martin put down his cup and took both of her hands in his.

"Oh Evie, I can't tell you enough what an honor that would be for me. To be able to walk down the aisle my sweet Evie whom I have been able to raise. But you know I can't."

Evie's eyes clouded with tears.

"But surely on such an occasion ..."

"No, dear one. First, a black man can't be with a white woman, even if I did raise you. And second, when pictures of us together hit the newspapers, why every person in Mississippi would know who we are. I bet some henchman would be here in New York within a day looking to lynch me and maybe you. Just know I'll be walking you down the aisle in spirit. OK?"

Evie nodded. "Some things are so unfair. But know you'll be in my heart. Since you can't escort me, I know what to do. I'll walk myself down the aisle. A bride walking alone is not unusual, and I will make a statement—I am beginning a new stage in my life."

Then Martin smiled. "I had a feeling you wanted to ask me to walk you down the aisle, so I made a trip to the bank. Look what I've kept for you all these years." He pulled out a velvet box from his coat pocket, opened it, and there before her was a beautiful pearl and diamond necklace with matching earrings. She carefully lifted them from the box, and then with tears in her eyes, she looked at Martin.

"Oh my. These are exquisite. Are they from the estate?"

"Yes, my dear one. With a note saying they were for your wedding and not before. This way, your parents and your grandparents will be with you in spirit too."

Evie reached up and gave her uncle a great big hug.

"I don't know how I could be so blessed, but I'm incredibly grateful. Thank you, Martin, for all you have done for me and for giving these to me."

Life took a different turn for Evie with so many changes. She wasn't working for the Ford Agency any longer and her role now with King's Department Store would be first as the owner's wife and then as an employee. She had so many people to thank. Eileen Ford had encouraged her to pursue King's, even though she wouldn't be able to model for them. If the Fords had never taken her in, she wouldn't have had the opportunity to meet King. Margie had supported her as a model and then as Queen of King's, never a jealous thought even when she became engaged to her boss. And Uncle Martin was always watching her back, always there for her.

Evie needed to make sure these people knew how much she appreciated them. So, she called Eileen Ford one day and invited her and her newest models over for dinner. Even though she was swamped with work and making decisions for the wedding, she had more time now than after the wedding. Maybe she could help some of the new models like she had been helped.

As for Margie and Uncle Martin, she wrote them both a letter, sharing her deepest thoughts, love, and appreciation for all they had done for her. As she dropped the letters in the mailbox, she felt blessed to have these wonderful loved ones in her life.

The weeks rolled into days until the weekend of the wedding was upon them. Evie and King wanted the Friday night before to be a celebration for all those who were a part of the wedding. After they had rehearsed in the church during the afternoon, King and Evie, Margie, and Thomas, along with Sara, and other close friends went to the Rainbow Room—one of Evie's and King's favorite places in New York. Rising sixty-five stories above Rockefeller Center, this famous restaurant had breathtaking skyline views. After dining on the delectable food, they danced to the music of a live band at the center of the iconic Crystal Ballroom.

As King pulled Evie up to dance, he whispered in her ear. "I know I am the luckiest man in all the world. To know you will be my wife and friend for the rest of my life is all I could ever want."

With tears in her eyes, she pulled his face close to her and kissed him with all the passion she couldn't keep inside. Yes, tomorrow was going to be epic. Tonight, holding each other as close as they could, love and happiness filled their hearts.

The next day went like clockwork and fortunately, there weren't any blackouts or problems. Evie and Margie got ready at the church in the bridal salon.

King and his best man, Thomas, would arrive early enough for pictures.

The only pictures that would wait until after the ceremony would be the ones of Evie and King. She didn't want him to see her until she walked down the aisle.

As Margie helped Evie with her dress, Sara joined them and there was much talking and squealing and laughter. When Margie pulled Evie's dress into position, the room became silent.

"Evie. I've never, ever seen you more beautiful in all the years I've known you," Margie said in an almost hushed whisper. "I knew this dress was beautiful, but I'm still blown away."

Evie agreed her gown was the loveliest she had ever seen. She and Sara had found three designer dresses they loved and combined their favorite parts of each into one dress made especially for Evie.

The dress was white satin with a shimmering, white silk overlay flowing to the floor with enough fabric to swish back and forth. Pearls, sequins, and tiny blush-colored roses covered the overlay. These roses were in beds of antique lace, dispersed intermittently throughout the dress as well as on the ten-foot train. The lights from the candles and lights caught the sequins edging the train.

The dress had long lace and pearl sleeves with the sleeve hem cut with a sharp point resting on her hand. The boat-neckline accented Evie's long neck and shoulders. The dress was tailored at the waist with the same white satin fabric but with lace overlay along the neckline and bodice. Then Margie clasped the heirloom necklace and stood back. Yes, Evie looked perfect.

Her bouquet was full of white, pink, and blush-pink roses and baby's breath. Evie's hair was in a French twist, and she wore a pearl and diamond tiara to match her necklace and earrings.

Everyone was speechless she was so beautiful. Margie opened a bottle of champagne, and the ladies toasted Evie and King and their future.

Margie lifted her glass. "The Lord knew I never needed a sister because he gave me Evie. I am so grateful to be here today, seeing you radiant in love on your wedding day. May you and King be blessed with God's wisdom, favor, and blessings in your marriage."

Sara agreed and lifted their glasses with smiles.

It was time to get in line for the walk to the foyer of the grand church and begin the long processional down the aisle.

Evie stood at the side of the foyer and watched the flower girls walk together, dropping fresh rose petals on the thick center aisle carpet while the organist played the beautiful music of Pachibel's Canon in D.

Before Margie started down the aisle, she looked at Evie. "I love you like a sister. No one, not even a husband, can separate us."

Moments later, Evie took a deep breath, paused at the sanctuary entrance as everyone rose and turned toward the back of the church when the traditional Bridal Chorus by Wagner began. Evie started her long walk to her beloved. Though the room was packed with friends and admirers, she saw only her King. They locked eyes and didn't stop looking at each other, even when she stood next to him, and the pastor began.

At the end of the ceremony, Evie handed her bouquet to Margie, then she and King walked up three steps and knelt on a velvet cushion for their first communion together as husband and wife.

When they moved back to their original position, the pastor spoke. "With great delight, I pronounce you husband and wife. You may kiss your bride."

King turned to face Evie, lifted the veil over her head, gently pulled her chin towards him and gave her a kiss they would both remember the rest of their lives.

They turned toward the congregation as the pastor announced, "I present to you, Mr. and Mrs. King Freeman."

King and Evie walked hand in hand down the aisle to a roar of applause. No one could mistake their smiles—these were two incredibly happy people.

After the pictures were taken, they got in a black limousine and drove to the wedding reception. They were thrilled they had chosen the beautiful Plaza Hotel with the grand ballroom large enough to hold all their guests. In fact, just this past November, in honor of the publisher Katherine Graham, the writer Truman Capote hosted his

"Black and White Ball" in the same grand ballroom. All of New York knew the only place to have a memorable party or reception would be at the Plaza.

The hotel was buzzing with photographers and people trying to see the famous couple. Hotel security, along with Martin, helped them into the hotel and to the ballroom. Their guests were already there, enjoying cocktails, champagne, and appetizers being passed around by smartly dressed waiters.

The tables for the sit-down dinner were magnificently decorated in flowing white tablecloths, gold and white covers for the chairs, candles dispersed everywhere, and flower arrangements that towered over every table, full of hundreds of flowers.

Evie's favorite were the "flower trees" that were placed all around the grand ballroom. Each tree had white cherry blossoms made of silk and covered fully. It made the room looked like a spring day. The trunk of each tree was entwined with ivy, and there were gold birdcages with tiny songbirds inside on each tree. Extra lights had been placed around the walls and flowed from the ceiling. The whole room truly looked magical.

Evie had wanted to spend time with King and her closest friends but she needed to spend most of the reception greeting the guests. At one point, King whispered in her ear, "Don't worry about not seeing me much during this reception—I'll make it up to you tonight," and gave her a kiss. The look they shared was totally understood by both.

The food was amazing, but Evie and King barely had time to eat any of it with all the toasting. So, one of the waiters made them a box to take with them. When the orchestra began playing, King took Evie out to the middle of the ballroom dance floor for the first dance.

Martin stood at the door, still working as the security detail, but never taking his eyes from his beloved Evie.

Margie joined him while they took in the sight of two people who were deeply in love as they danced.

"I still can't believe Evie is married," Margie said. "I've known her since we were in grade school, and she's grown up and married."

"I can't believe it either, Margie. When I think about how little she was when we first came here from Mississippi and how scared she was in this here big city, well I can't believe she's now a grown woman, married."

As Martin remembered where Evie had come from, he knew this marriage was nothing short of a miracle.

CHAPTER THIRTEEN

Near midnight, King whispered in her ear, "I'm ready to leave. How about you?"

Evie nodded and smiled. "I'm ready too. I think we've talked to everyone. I want to be with just you." He leaned down and kissed her, then took her hand and led her off the dance floor. The party was still going strong, but they'd had enough. It was time for just the two of them.

Evie threw her bouquet to the single ladies, aiming, of course, toward Margie, said goodbye to all, and was whisked to the waiting limo. Everyone waved and threw rice. As King began to help Evie into the limousine, he leaned down and kissed her. The crowd went wild. Then he got in the car and the limousine headed out toward 5th Avenue. However, as it turned the corner, the limo turned toward a back entrance to the hotel.

"Why are we going back to the Plaza?" Evie asked.

"Because we're going to spend our first night in its famous and beautiful Wedding Suite. I knew we'd be exhausted from the day and didn't need to travel to some other place. This suite will literally overwhelm you, Evie. I can hardly wait to see your face when we walk in."

A staff member opened the back door and led them to an unnoticed elevator where he punched "Penthouse Floor" on the keypad. Slowly, they began their ascent. When the elevator doors opened, the first thing Evie saw was soft rose petals trailing from the elevator door to the massive mahogany double doors at the end of the hallway. The bellhop gave King the key and got back into the elevator.

"Well, love, it's just you and me. Let's walk to those doors and see if this key fits." As King put in the brass key, the doors opened. He swept Evie up in his arms and crossed the threshold. "I know this isn't our home, but for the next two days, it will be. What do you think of the Bridal Suite?"

Evie gasped. She couldn't believe any room could be this beautiful. Rose petals were everywhere on the deep carpet, leading up to the massive, canopied king-sized bed. Lighted candles stood on every open space and cast a soft, romantic glow on the room. Someone had lit a fire in the marble fireplace sending out warmth to the room. On the opposite side of the room, a small sofa nestled near a gold and glass table with a crystal ice bucket on top, filled with a bottle of champagne and a bowl of chocolate strawberries.

The bathroom was at the other end. Never had Evie seen so much marble—marble floor, marble-footed bathtub, marble shower with two shower heads, and marble sinks with gold faucets. Her makeup case had already been opened and placed next to one of the sinks, and the closet was filled with the clothes from her suitcase. Margie or Sara or someone had gone to a lot of trouble to ensure she wouldn't have to lift a finger and would feel genuinely like a queen.

There was also a velvet chaise lounge in the marble bathroom next to another fireplace, lit, of course, where her white satin wedding night peignoir set was laid. And candles were flickering everywhere here too.

"Oh, King! I love everything about the suite. Thank you for giving me such a beautiful wedding but, especially, such a beautiful room for our bridal night."

"My pleasure, and to see your face this happy made my plan worthwhile. This is a beautiful room for sure. And the marble in the bathroom? That's straight from the Italian quarry in Carrara where Michelangelo obtained his marble. Let's sit by the fireplace, drink some champagne, and talk about the wedding."

Still in her gorgeous wedding dress, Evie glided over to the sofa, slipping off her shoes. Over glasses of champagne and strawberries, they shared the highlights from the day.

"Do you know when I first fell in love with you?" King asked as he cuddled her close. "The day you wore the wedding dress in one of your first fashion shows at the store. You had such a smile on your face, and then as you began your turn, our eyes met. I knew in that instant I wanted you in my life, even though I was already engaged to Vanessa. I tried to forget that moment, but fate thought otherwise."

"I so remember that day! I almost forgot to keep walking when I saw you. But there was even an earlier time when I became enchanted with you, dear husband. Martin showed me around the store when I graduated from modeling school. You walked into the fashion area, and he introduced us. You took my hand, looked at me straight in the eyes, and talked to me. I don't think I washed that hand for a week."

"I remember that! Isn't it funny how our memories are different? I thought you were too young and too beautiful to want to meet me. Life is so strange at times."

Evie smiled and brought his hand to her heart. "Life may be strange but what a blessing. Knowing we are together for the rest of our lives is nothing short of a miracle. A girl from back woods Mississippi and a marketing tycoon from New York City are married now."

They continued enjoying the champagne and reminiscing about their day. Evie moved to the side of the sofa, stretched her bare feet on King's lap, and he massaged them. Talking and reminiscing about the day was fun, but soon she was yawning. King kissed her and asked if she wanted to get ready for bed.

"Yes, I'm so tired! And ... a little nervous."

"I know you may be, but, Evie, don't worry about a thing. I cherish and take care of those I love, and you are the one person I love more than anyone or anything in the world. I promise, tonight will be a beautiful expression of our love, even if we just lie there and hold each other. You will know when the time is right for us to be one. There is no need to rush or hurry."

Evie hugged him with all her might. Her lips reached for his in a kiss of true love and trust. She knew he would be understanding, but to hear him tell her was wonderful.

As she came out from the bathroom in her beautiful satin nightgown and robe, King was already in bed. He reached out for her. She came to him quickly and nestled next to his warm body. As he leaned in to kiss her softly on her lips, she knew she had nothing to fear.

CHAPTER FOURTEEN

Their honeymoon was everything Evie had dreamed. After spending two nights at the Plaza, with their meals brought to them by room service, their limousine took them to New York harbor where they got on the Trans-Atlantic steamship, the *Queen Elizabeth*, bound for Europe. The *QE* was a wonderful ship, with understated British luxury.

Their stateroom consisted of a living room, bedroom, bathroom, and balcony.

"How do you like the room?" asked King as they began to unpack their luggage.

"I had no idea there were rooms this large or grand on a ship! I love looking out the window and seeing the water and blue sky."

They were gone for a month, touring either by train, boat, or car, starting by visiting London, Paris, and Rome. They visited grand castles and museums, saw breathtaking views, and beautifully laid out gardens—their favorite was Versailles. They needed two days to see the rooms inside the palace and the gardens and fountains outside.

They were blessed with perfect weather as they walked hand and hand around the many gardens that composed the whole area. Neither could believe how large and spectacular these were with manicured bushes, trees, and fountains covering an area of almost two thousand acres. It was known as one of the biggest gardens in the world.

Evie and King sat on one of the ivy-covered benches in an open-air room with a grass and pebble floor resembling a ballroom. It was magnificent.

"Can you believe one king had the foresight to build such an estate? What is your favorite place here, Evie?"

"Oh, that's easy. Marie Antoinette's retreat—the *Hameau de la Reine*—or, as we would say at home, the Queen's Hamlet. From what I've read, she craved for a private escape from all the stress of being Queen of France. She was supposed to entertain the courtiers daily. So, her husband, King Louis XVI, built the small home for her. She could wear simple clothes and her children could run and play in the yard."

"I agree. The palace is amazing, but it would be filled with people. I read in the pamphlet that, depending on the day, there were between three thousand and ten thousand people here, forming a highly variegated society. I'd hate to have to be around so many. The royal couple even had to eat their meals in front of the top courtesans. Yes, I'd want to build a private retreat. With you in it of course!"

The small retreat was Evie's favorite place at Versailles because Marie Antoinette reminded her somewhat of herself. She was just a young girl when she married the future king of France and left her family, home, and all she had ever known to live in another country with a new language, customs, and people. She'd had such a hard time fitting in, and court life was full of rituals and traditions. In her smaller, private home on the property, Marie could be herself. She had cows and chickens and gardens, so she and her children and attendants could eat normal food and be on their own schedule.

That's how I hope King and I will be able to live when we get back home. With all the demands on him, I hope he will feel our home is a haven.

Leaving France, they made their way to Austria and the city of Vienna, Marie Antoinette's home. How sad for her to marry a French King for the purpose of uniting their two countries only to die by the guillotine. One highlight of Vienna was attending an opera at the famous Vienna State Opera House. They then traveled through Germany and into Switzerland. There was plenty of snow, which made their visit more magical, especially seeing the snow-covered mountains and the Matterhorn. They also visited the city of Lucerne, considered one of the prettiest cities in the world with the Chapel Bridge and the Water Tower. Their last stop was to the south of France where they visited the Prince and Princess Rainer of Monaco who had been married a little over ten years before them and had come to the King's grand banquets earlier.

Finally, they boarded their ship for the slow but wonderful trip back to the States and real life. On their last night on board, they decided to skip the formal dinner and instead ordered room service and ate off a tray in bed.

"Now this is the way to eat dinner," King said as he gently touched his wine glass to hers. "Let's never get so busy or set in a routine that we forget to just be us."

"I totally agree, my husband. Dinner in bed is a future must do."

Martin was waiting for them with a limousine when they arrived in New York and filled them in on the latest news on the store. Fortunately, all was fine, and not too many problems had occurred while they were gone.

"I sure hope y'all had a grand time. Everyone sure missed you though." Martin loaded their suitcases into the trunk of the limo. "Evie, here's some mail I brought. You can open it once we get you home." Martin had a strange look on his face, so Evie put the letter in her purse.

"Martin, please take us to the townhouse," King said. "I can hardly wait to be home with my wife."

Martin turned around and tipped his cap. "Yes, sir. I know you can't. And, Evie, you will be delighted to know all the redecorations you wanted are finished, and a special guest is already there."

"Who?"

"Why Princess of course! You didn't want to come back to your new home without her, did you?"

Evie squealed. "Oh, I can't wait to see it all. Thank you for letting me know and for having Princess there when we arrive." She turned to King. "I can't wait for us to see our new home together today."

King and Evie had discussed building their own home with her ideas and designs, but his townhouse was close to the store, already beautifully decorated, and had a fabulous kitchen. Although they might build in the future, at this point, he told her she could redecorate any of the rooms she desired. She chose two rooms to focus on: the glassed-in solarium and one of the bedrooms next to the master bedroom. She wanted these rooms decorated while they were gone, so they were ready by the time they returned. After the long honeymoon, Evie was glad she had moved most of her items to the townhome before they had left, because she was exhausted. Leaving Margie and their magical apartment had been hard, but fortunately Sara took her place in the apartment.

Evie's mind was on the letter Martin had handed to her.

"I can't believe we're finally home," said Evie as the car turned into the driveway. "I think I'd like to go straight upstairs and take a bath. OK, honey? Then we can go tour the newly decorated rooms."

"Sure, go on ahead. Martin and I can get the luggage upstairs in a bit. I need to go through my mail, so I'll go straight to my office. Let me know when you want something to eat and for the tour."

Evie rushed upstairs and quickly opened the letter Martin had handed to her.

Evie, I didn't want to wait another day to give you this information. I hope King doesn't find this letter. After you two left the wedding reception, a man came up to me. Asked me my name and where I had come from. Said I looked familiar and that he was looking for someone who might be my family. Of course, I gave him a false name and said I was from Georgia, but I don't trust him. He had come with a friend of King's who had been invited. Said he'd been hired by some people down South to find this person a few years back.

Evie, he sure scared me. In the back of my mind, I've thought someone might look for us, but I really didn't believe anyone would. Why would anyone be looking for us now after all these years? All I can think of is someone is out for blood and is putting up some blood money. I don't want you to worry or be scared 'cause I haven't seen anyone since. But I wanted you to know before you came back to the store. If anyone approaches you, make up some good lies and come looking for me. All my love, M

Evie drew a deep breath and said a silent prayer. If Martin was scared, this could be serious. But she'd been gone from Mississippi such a long time, she decided to burn the letter and not worry. She sure didn't want King to know, though. Anyway, a bath should take away all thoughts of someone wanting to hurt her or Martin.

Evie hated having to keep anything from King. But she knew she couldn't share why Martin protected her and tried to keep her safe. Only Evie knew the threat was still out there. Even though she and King had made a promise to never keep secrets from each other, to always be truthful and speak the truth in love, she'd made her first promise to Uncle Martin. Keeping this one secret hidden forever from King would be hard. But Martin knew best, and she had already promised him she would never tell anyone her secret. Inside, though, she felt terrible hiding anything from King.

To calm her mind, Evie relaxed in the tub and thought back to the day she'd taken Margie on a tour of King's townhouse and shown her the two rooms where she needed Margie's design help.

"Margie, would you believe this townhouse has six bedrooms and bathrooms? I want to show you each one—especially the bedroom I want to redecorate. I'd love some of your design ideas. I also want you to see King's study/library, the formal areas, and my favorite—the kitchen, small dining room, and family den which is where we will spend most of our time."

As they walked through the impressive home, Margie expressed delight in everything. "Evie, decorating always excites me. I hope I can come up with some good ideas."

"Oh, Margie, I'm sure you will. Now, this is the first room I want to decorate—the solarium. I want this to be a peaceful refuge. Since it's next to the family dining room where we will eat breakfast, I will spend time there after King goes to the office. He goes to work much earlier than I do so I will covet this quiet time. As you can see, the room is circular and has a vaulted ceiling. I was thinking of painting the room white with a blue ceiling, like the sky. Don't you just love all the windows? Sunlight can filter in most of the day."

"I love the openness. You must have white wicker furniture—sofas, chairs, and a chaise lounge. It would be like a Southern screened porch! Buy lots of glass top tables for your books and flowerpots full of every type of plant. We can get a beautiful chintz fabric in that fabric store we love so much. It has all the colors you love—pinks, yellows, blues, and lavender along with patterns of flowers and birds. Oh, Evie, this room will be magnificent—like an English garden but inside."

"Do you really think so, Margie? Your opinion means so much. Ok, ready for the last room?"

"I can't wait, but I'm already loving this house and wanting to move in," she said with a laugh.

They walked upstairs to the second floor where Evie first showed her the master bedroom.

"I love the master suite, but it's quite masculine. The furniture is solid mahogany and as you can see, the walls are covered in beige, grasscloth wallpaper. The hardwood floors are covered in dark oriental rugs. So, when King said I could change any of the rooms, I decided on turning one of the bedrooms into a room for myself: A bedroom/office combination. A bedroom that is much more feminine where I can sleep when King is out of town and an office to give me a place where I can manage the household business. I really need your design ideas."

Evie turned to the next bedroom—an empty but large and spacious room. Only a pastel Chinese carpet lay on the white pine floors with a chandelier above.

The room, on the east side of the building receiving the morning sun, had lots of windows and a balcony overlooking the park.

"I'd like to have it painted a robin egg blue with white trim. As you can see, along the raised ceiling is dentil molding which is quite stunning. The floors are in great condition, and I love the carpet."

"Oh Evie, I love this room! And yes, to have your own special place would be wonderful. I think you should get a queen-sized canopy bed with a pale blue velvet headboard to match the walls. Then add large billowy white silk canopy drapes flowing down to pool on the floor. Remember that antique store we went to last week? There was a perfect country French bedside table in white with a mirror top. And I'd have lights installed next to the headboard so you can read in bed. I've always wanted lights by my bed. The chandelier hanging in the center of the room appears to be Italian glass and is perfect for you."

Evie could imagine the room just as Margie explained.

"Margie, I love all your ideas. And did you notice the fireplace? I want to add a chaise lounge next to it with a small table for my books. You know I can't live without my books. I'll place a small desk on the other side of the fireplace."

"Yes, I love that idea. And I'd add a low chest against that other wall where you can place your silver brush set, perfumes, and maybe have a vase with flowers. Oh Evie, the room will be heavenly."

"And the best part? The balcony. Look at that view. Hopefully, we can find a small table and chairs or even rocking chairs. Margie, I'm going to love opening these French doors wide and letting the sun and breeze in. And this room is where you can spend the night any time you want."

"Evie, really? That makes me so happy. I guess I haven't lost you after all."

"You'll never lose me, Margie. Never."

Evie brought her thoughts back to the present when the bath water became tepid. She wrapped up in a pale pink robe and decided now was the time to see the newly decorated rooms with King. Princess hadn't left her side since she got home and had fallen asleep on the soft bathroom rug next to the bathtub.

"Princess, ready to tour your new home?" Evie scooped up the cat in her arms and headed downstairs to King's office.

"King, are you ready to tour our new home?"

"Yes. I've caught up on mail, and I can hardly wait to see what you and Margie have come up with. But I know I'll love every idea."

As Evie and King viewed the new rooms together, Evie felt like she had finally come home after all the years of being an orphan.

"I love what you have accomplished, love," said King. "The furniture, the colors, the fabrics all look like you. Thank you for making our home so beautiful."

"You couldn't make me happier now that I know you love the rooms. We will have many, many wonderful years together in this home." Evie reached up to touch King's face and gave him a kiss. "How blessed we are."

Later that night as Evie got ready for bed, she thought about her husband, her home, her friends, her job, and the rest of her life. Things couldn't get any better than this. Everything was perfect. God had blessed her beyond imagination and her thankfulness overflowed.

CHAPTER FIFTEEN

Evie stayed home the first week after their honeymoon to finish settling in, but now she was ready to get back to work. She and King had met many of the owners of the great stores in Europe, as well as many suppliers. Her notebook was full of the many ideas from their trip and she could hardly wait to share them at the staff meeting on Monday.

The staff greeted her with smiles when the meeting began at nine.

"Evie, I know you have many ideas you wanted to share this morning," King said. "So, please go ahead."

She gave him a warm smile. "Thanks. As you all know, last year we had decided to bring in some well-known actors, authors, adventurers, and so on, and link them with the fashions and novelty items we have at the store. So far, only a few have been here. I'd like to make a list of people we could invite, and I need your help."

Thomas spoke up immediately. "Let's invite the Beatles to perform. We'd have a full store."

Everyone cracked up.

"OK, that would be a miracle, Thomas," King said. "Evie, any other ideas?"

Evie spoke up. "Well, along with Thomas's idea of bringing in famous singers, we could bring in Cher and showcase our fashions around some of the 'pop' clothes she loves to wear. Or, along that train of thought, we could invite the model, Twiggy. She could be part of a fashion show."

"Maybe we could invite Julie Andrews?" suggested another executive.

"I think she would be really hard to get," Evie said. "However, what about Heloise? She writes *Heloise's Housekeeping Hints,* and we could have her speak to the ladies from our housewares department."

King looked up. "Great idea! Any others?"

Mrs. Howard, King's personal secretary, had an idea. "My grandchildren love books by Charles Schulz. He could read aloud in the children's section. You'd have them, plus all their moms, in the store, and I'm sure they would buy quite a lot."

"I love that idea," King said. "And perhaps we could bring in Anne Morrow Lindbergh. Although she wrote *Dearly Beloved* a few years ago, I know our women customers would come in to hear her speak. She's an American institution."

"Thank you, King, and everyone," Evie said. "You have given me a list of great potential guests. I think we're off to a great start. I'll keep you posted as the events get formalized."

The staff meeting continued with other items they needed to discuss and then adjourned. King and Evie went up to the Tea Room for lunch and finished talking about other ideas. All things considered, her first day back was a pleasure.

Summer came fast with high temperatures and even higher humidity. The store continued to keep pace with current events, as well as bring in some of the celebrities they had discussed. Evie and King couldn't have been happier. Their love for each other was evident and that love and caring filtered throughout the store. The employees felt in partnership with King's and were never afraid to offer any suggestion to either King or Evie. Evie loved her position there. She was able to work with the senior staff, as well as the clerks in all the departments. And she could still model, which was her passion, along with helping plan the fashion shows for King's.

Even better, Evie could see Margie and Martin as much as she wanted and she felt, for the first time ever, as though she had a real family. Martin still had his eyes peeled and ears open in case that man who asked questions at the wedding reception came back. But nothing had materialized, and from what Martin had told Evie, he decided the threat was gone. At least for now.

As summer transitioned into fall, the brisk air was refreshing, but then winter came roaring in with an early snowstorm. All of New York was taken unaware. By New Year's Eve 1968, Evie and King celebrated being together almost a full year. And for Valentine's they went back to the Plaza and stayed in the Bridal Suite for their anniversary— one of the sweetest times in their young marriage.

By the end of February, Evie decided she needed to go with Sara, who was now head of the Lady's Couture Department, to Paris to help with the buying. Leaving King was a hard decision, but Evie believed with the combination of the two of them, they would be able to see more fashions and help each other with buying decisions. By the time they arrived back in New York, they were exhausted but also thrilled at the inventory they bought. The ladies of New York would not be able to resist the new fashions.

Evie also couldn't wait to get back to the store. Even though she could have gone home and unpacked and rested, she had to see King and tell him she was back in the States. She wanted to fill him in on everything they had accomplished. Since the plane got in early, she decided to surprise him, rather than calling first. So, Evie and Sara found a limo at the airport and went straight to King's.

As the car approached the city, the conditions of the streets shocked Evie. She'd heard about the garbage strike while in Paris, but this? The city looked like a vast slum as mounds of refuse were piled high. The wind whirled the filth throughout the streets. She stopped the limo to buy a newspaper and read that about thirty thousand tons of trash was on the streets, a number the reporter thought would grow to over a hundred thousand. The garbage was piled chest high. Eggs shells, coffee grounds, milk cartons, uneaten food, and empty beer cans littered the sidewalks.

Fortunately, their limo could take them straight to the front door of King's. When they arrived, Evie rode up the elevator. As she reached King's office, she put a finger to her mouth and smiled at Mrs. Howard. As she headed into King's office, he was speaking with someone she had never met before.

"Evie! You're back! I'm so glad you're here." He walked over to her and gave her a big hug and kiss. "You surprised me, but I'm thrilled you did. I thought you were getting in late tonight. I've missed you too much and have been waiting for your call." He hugged and kissed her again. As they drew apart, he introduced the man he had been speaking with.

"Evie, this is Hunter Wallace. He just came over from Marshall's in Chicago with glowing reviews, and we've hired him to begin working with our Marketing Department. He has some great ideas on how to increase sales, etc. Hunter, this is my wife, Evie."

As she shook his hand, she felt a wave of coldness come over her. "How do you do?

"Very well." Hunter smiled. "I've heard so much about King's, his famous banquets, and the specialty items he seems to procure as no one else in the industry can. I've really enjoyed working this last week."

Though this new associate smiled, all Evie could see was his slicked black hair and dark, black eyes. A feeling of apprehension swept over her.

"Thank you for your kind words. King, I do need to go over a few things with you regarding my trip," Evie said. "Is now all right or should I come back? I don't want to interrupt."

"Yes, don't let me keep you, King," Hunter said. "We'll catch up at the club tonight. Evie, a delight." He left.

Evie and King hugged, kissed, and then held on to each other a moment.

"I've missed my Evie so much. I think this is the last time you go on a trip without me."

"I agree. I won't leave without you next time. But I can't wait to tell you all about the trip and the items we bought for the store." Evie sat down in her usual chair. "But before I tell you about my trip, how did you decide to hire this man? You just met him and have already hired him? I'm a little confused. I thought our marketing department was perfect."

"I believed the department was great but to tell you the truth, meeting Hunter changed my mind. I got a call from a friend, James, who was at our wedding, who said Hunter would be coming by for an interview and that we shouldn't let him go. I met him, was impressed, and decided on the spur of the moment to hire him. He's starting as a basic hire until I can see what he can do. But from his recommendations, I think he will rise to the top. He's already made some great suggestions with our personnel and strategy. Are you upset that I did?"

"You have good instincts about your store, and you need to follow them. It's just that hiring him happened so fast. You don't know anything about him. I just hope ..."

"You hope what?"

"Oh, nothing. I hope hiring him isn't a mistake. My woman's intuition is prodding me. But you know best in these situations. Do you really have to go out with him tonight? I just got home."

"Well, honey, I wasn't expecting you until later tonight. We need to meet to discuss some items where we won't be interrupted. I promise I'll make it up to you when I get home."

Though she still wasn't sure about Hunter, she dismissed her thoughts and told King about her trip, saying how the buying she did would be beneficial for the store. But he didn't seem to be listening—he couldn't keep his hands off her. It was so good to be back home with him.

"I'm going to go home and unpack, then get some rest. By the way, does this awful garbage strike affect the store?"

"Not sure because the strike just started. We're experiencing less traffic in the store. Our customers don't want to get out and shop with all this garbage." As King kissed her again, he murmured how much he loved her.

She had a hard time leaving him, but she pried herself away. As she headed toward the front door of the store, she noticed new people working. Some of the regular staff were gone. On her way out, she spotted Uncle Martin at the front door, and after saying how much they missed each other, she asked if he noticed a difference.

"I do see some changes, but I'm afraid to talk about anything right now."

"Afraid? What does that mean?

"Let's talk about this later." Martin glanced over both shoulders.

"I want you and Margie to come to my house tonight for dinner. I've missed both of you so much while I was gone. I'm still on European time and I won't be able to sleep till late. Margie called me while I was gone—said she's having such a struggle in her new position with the marketing department. She said she needed to talk to me when I got back. King will be at the club with a new employee, Hunter, so we can all speak freely."

"Well, I'd love that, Evie, I sure would. Thank you."

She made her way to one of the floor phones and called Mrs. B to see if she had time to cook for company. She reassured her and said to come home soon and tell her all about Paris. Evie also called Margie who, of course, squealed when she heard Evie's voice and found out she was back home.

As she turned back toward the front door, Evie thought again about her conversation with Uncle Martin. What on earth was making him afraid to talk at work? Then she spotted Hunter. Oh, that man gave her the creeps. She could hear him talk to Martin.

"Boy, I need the door opened for me!"

Boy! He's calling Martin 'boy'? Evie made a beeline for the front door.

Martin calmly opened the door but kept his body and head erect, not paying any homage to Hunter.

"I don't know why on earth King keeps him around," Evie heard Hunter say under his breath as he stalked out of the store.

"Martin, what's going on?" Evie asked.

Martin looked at her with great sadness. "Nothing for you to worry your sweet face about. Sometimes people just forget to be nice."

"I've never heard such disrespect! I'm going to mention this to King."

"Don't do that! It will work itself out. The best thing you and I can do is ignore it. Now, you get on home and I'll see you tonight. Sure is kind of you to invite me over for a good meal and a visit with you. Both will make me feel better."

Evie left the store, but her heart was troubled. How could anyone talk to her Martin that way?

Joy flooded her when she saw her dear Margie and Martin at her front door later.

"I'm so happy you both could come tonight. How I've missed getting together like we used to. Come on in and let me take your coats. Mrs. B has really done up dinner for us tonight. We aren't going to be fancy," Evie said when she saw the confusion in their eyes as they passed through the unprepared dining room. "We're going to eat at the family table. Come on through this way."

There next to the large kitchen was the beautiful white pine table with colorful table mats, napkins, plates, and the lazy Susan covered in hot dishes of food—fried chicken, a ham, sweet potato casserole, green beans, black-eyed peas, buttermilk biscuits with plenty of fresh butter and honey, and a pitcher of iced tea on the sideboard.

"Oh, Evie, this looks like heaven," Margie said. "I can't believe you and Mrs. B made all of this scrumptious food."

"You can take home leftovers for your lunches and dinners tomorrow. I remember the difficulty of making our sack lunches, Margie. Now let's sit down, dig in, and enjoy being together. I'm eager to hear all the news."

They enjoyed eating so much they could hardly talk. When they were finished, Mrs. B brought in the cherry cobbler with vanilla ice cream and poured hot coffee for each one. The cobbler was warm enough to melt the ice cream, which made the whole dessert heavenly.

"Let's take our coffee to the family room, which is a much cozier place to catch up and talk."

Martin and Margie settled on the two chairs matching the sofa Evie chose.

"So, what's going on at the store?" Evie asked as she curled her feet under her. "I want all the details—leave nothing out."

Margie and Martin looked at each other.

Margie began. "After you left for Paris, the new man, Hunter Wallace, started 'taking over.' I mean he was with King every day, going into the offices and talking to all the personnel, and within a few days, people started leaving.

I feel lucky I still have a job. The whole atmosphere at the store is totally different."

"I don't see how one person can cause this much change. Martin?"

Martin sighed and took a long breath. "The whole problem boils down to one thing—this man isn't good, isn't good at all. Somehow, he has King's ear. He's with him all the time. Sadly, he's disrespectful of most of the employees—especially the colored ones. All of us are having a hard time."

Evie was speechless. "Have King and Hunter been going to the club a lot? That's where they are tonight. I thought they were having a meeting."

"All the time," Martin said. "And King doesn't even listen to his executive staff anymore. The only one who advises King is Hunter. It's like King has been taken over by some strange force. I don't know what we should do."

"I don't know either, but I'll get to the bottom of this. It doesn't make sense. Thank you for trusting me and letting me know what's going on."

They switched subjects, enjoying their time together until time for Margie and Martin to leave. And for Evie to find out what in the world was going on.

CHAPTER SIXTEEN

Evie was still awake when King came home that night. She wanted to have time to talk to him and see if he might share anything that might give her a clue as to what was going on.

He seemed so happy to see her and was thrilled she was awake. They talked about nothing and everything. Finally, Evie asked him about Hunter.

"Tell me about this new employee, Hunter. Does he have good ideas?"

"Good ideas? You can't imagine! I don't know how I've managed all these years without him. King's will only get better because of him."

"One man can make that much difference?"

"You just wait and see, my Evie. I think you will feel the same way as I do." Then he changed the subject. "I've missed you too much." He leaned in to kiss her with such passion that she forgot there was anything to worry about.

The next few weeks troubled Evie as she could see the way Hunter talked and treated anyone who was colored. While she was setting up for the Tea Room fashion show, Hunter came into the room and told some of the colored help to leave. He even went backstage where the models were getting their assignments and told one of the colored models to leave. Evie protested but Hunter came up with some wild story that she had done something wrong and he had to let her go for "the good of the store."

Then reports began trailing into her office about the way he treated Martin. In fact, everyone could tell he despised Martin more than anyone at the store. They had little choice but to honor Hunter, though, because they wanted to keep their jobs. Martin, on the other hand, would not. He did his job but would not bow down to Hunter the way everyone else did. But how long would that last?

As Evie walked through King's on a busy Saturday, she could sense that the joy and excitement were gone. Saturdays usually were everyone's favorite day and had a special feeling due to the increase in customers and sales. But today, the clerks kept their heads down when working at their stations, and not one of them was smiling. As Evie said hi to them, they glanced up, barely smiled, and went about their work. The situation was the same in the couture section of the store but at least the salesladies there would talk to her.

"Evie, it's so good to see you! Please stay here. Don't go back to your office. You're the only ray of sunshine we have."

"That makes me feel good. Thanks. But what's going on? No one has talked to me as I walked through the store."

Two of the ladies looked at each other. "Everything is different, Miss Evie, since that Hunter showed up."

One of the ladies pinched her and stopped talking.

"Please don't be afraid to talk to me."

"Since Hunter came on the scene, we're afraid we may lose our jobs. He criticizes everyone and everything. We've lost some of our best employees, and the store just isn't the same. I'm worried."

"Let me see what I can do," Evie said. "I'm glad you spoke up."

If the sales staff was afraid even to talk about what was troubling them, this situation was getting out of hand. She had some ideas about the next author she wanted to invite to the store for a presentation and decided this was the perfect time to go talk to King.

Evie marched toward King's office with her notebook and file in hand.

"Mrs. Howard, is King in?

"I don't think you can go in right now."

"Why not?" Evie took a few steps toward the door. "I can always go in, you know that."

As Evie opened the door, she saw King and Hunter hunched over some paperwork and whispering to one another. When Hunter looked up, he scowled, but when he saw Evie, he appeared to paste on a smile, though not a warm one.

"Evie, love, what brings you here?" King said. "We're kind of busy now."

"I wanted to talk to you about our next author event. Remember, we invited Anne Morrow Lindbergh to come and discuss her *Dearly Beloved* book? I've brought my notebook and her file to show you."

"Yes, yes, I remember we had that on the agenda. Let's talk later, OK? I'll drop by your office this afternoon." King resumed talking to Hunter, who turned his back on her.

Evie was stunned. She turned and shut the door behind her. King had never brushed her off like that. She was going to do some talking that afternoon.

But King never did make it to her office that day, which greatly troubled her. So, Evie took all her notes home with her. Fortunately, King was there for dinner.

"Let's go in the family room with our coffee," Evie said after their meal. She kicked off her shoes and curled up on the sofa.

King sat next to her, which was a relief. She finally had him all to herself. Maybe this situation with Hunter would work itself out.

"You never made it to my office today, so I brought my notes home. Here's what I was thinking we should do in the ladies' Fine Dress Department. We can set up a small bookstore with Anne Lindbergh's books stacked around a fake fireplace, small rug, and chairs for the ladies. What do you think?"

"That sounds like a great idea. You take it and run with it. Hunter and I have lots of work to do, so I won't be able to help you much with this."

Evie dropped her notebook on the coffee table. "But I need you to introduce Anne and be there to greet everyone who attends."

"Can't do it this time. You don't understand how much I must do now. Hunter has great plans for our future."

"Excuse me? *Our* future? Does that mean you and me or you and Hunter?"

"Now don't get hysterical. Any plan for King's that succeeds is a plan for us. I don't understand why you're so negative about Hunter. What has he ever done to you?"

Evie stared at King. "For one thing, he's changed my husband. And he's changed the entire atmosphere of the store. And worse, he hates the colored, especially Martin. Do you know how many people he has fired? Or how poorly he treats Martin?"

King stood, jostling the coffee table, and grabbed his paperwork on it. "Hunter has already explained to me that with the people he's fired, more money will come into the store. He laid the figures all out for me and what he says makes sense. I'm not sure where all this dissent and argument is coming from but I'm going back to the office. You clearly don't know what you're talking about or the intense inner workings of the store. And you don't understand how important Hunter is to the store. I don't want us to get in a fight, so I need to leave."

He left Evie in a state of despair. They had never fought like that, and she didn't know what to do. Stunned, she went up to her own bedroom and sobbed.

By the time King got to his office, he had cooled down somewhat. *Maybe I should call Evie and apologize?* But then just thinking about their fight made him mad all over again. Why couldn't she just accept his decisions? And Hunter? King's was *his* store, and he knew more about running the place than she did. And Hunter had shown him, on paper, how much more money the store could make if he was able to implement his plans. And the more money Hunter could make for the store, the bigger the store could get.

He tossed his notes on the desk, got some coffee, and crashed down in his large leather chair. He was mad and irritated, but he wasn't sure why. Maybe because Evie dared to question his judgment.

As he started to organize his papers, he saw Evie's notebook. He remembered the time Evie came to her first staff meeting. She was afraid but also ready to tackle the challenge of working at King's. She was just so stinking cute, especially when she started to take notes, as if she were still in school. Then he asked to see her notebook and was surprised. She had taken some terrific notes of the entire meeting and added some of her own thoughts and ideas on the margins. He had been impressed.

He leaned back in his chair and opened the notebook which was like a diary of his store, a full account of all the goings-on. He turned a few pages and saw one item recorded that was underlined in red ink. "Martin Johnson, head of security, reported that some men who had come into the store were actually there to survey and plan an attack on King himself, as well as the store. Fortunately, he contacted the FBI who were able to recognize them and keep an eye out. Sure enough, they were caught stealing drugs and were now in jail. If not for the quick work of Mr. Johnson, King could have been killed. The courts found the men were part of a Mafia ring and wanted to take over the store as a front for their operations."

Then there was another message in the margin that Evie had added. "I'm forever indebted to Martin for keeping my King safe!" That made King smile. Evie cared for him even then.

A few hours later, he fell asleep on his sofa.

Over dinner, Hunter's wife, Zera, toasted him, "To the man of my dreams who will make all our dreams come true."

Hunter and their friends agreed and offered more toasts in his honor. He couldn't contain his excitement that he was technically the number two man at King's. He bragged about his income, his great family that included five sons, and his future success.

"The only thing that can mar my feelings of success is thinking about that Martin Johnson," Hunter said. "He's disrespectful to me and acts like he owns the place. I don't know what to do to get rid of him."

"Why not ask King tomorrow morning if you could relocate Martin to another store for the purpose of learning more about security?" Zera put the part about security in air quotes. "You told me King's and Marshall Field's in Chicago help each other. You could get rid of him for now, then examine everything he'd done as the head of security. Surely you can find some misdeed on his part—one that would allow you to involve the authorities. Then he could be thrown in jail."

"My darling, Zera. You are magnificent. Best idea I've heard of all day. I'll go in early in the morning and talk to King right away. After Martin is gone, I'll hire my own security who will be more, let's say, favorable toward me. Let's toast this new plan and our future without Martin!"

After his guests left, Hunter stayed up all night. He couldn't sleep as he paced back and forth, devising his plan.

His pacing woke Zera. "You may as well go on to work. Call me with the good news after Martin is gone."

At six o'clock, Hunter arrived at the store, all smiles and ready to work. He was surprised to see King already there but that made it easier to talk to him.

"Hunter, what are you doing here so early?"

"Oh, I couldn't sleep, and I can see you couldn't either. My wife told me I might as well head into work, so here I am."

King sat up from the sofa and rubbed the sleep from his eyes. "Well, I'm glad you're here. I realized last night I had forgotten to honor one of the employees. Maybe a promotion and a bonus? If I wanted to honor someone, what do you think I should do?"

Hunter practically jumped out of his skin with excitement. He was going to get promoted! "I'm glad you asked. I think, to really pay tribute to someone, you should have a meeting with all your employees. Ask this person to come and stand next to you, then share with everyone what he has done. Give him a plaque, which will be hung somewhere prominent in the store. Perhaps take an ad out in the *New York Times* with his picture and what he has done. And then, of course, give him a promotion and a wonderful bonus. What do you think?"

"You never fail me. When the store opens, go get Martin Johnson, head of security. He's the one I want to acknowledge. He saved my life last year and I never thanked him. Go to the marketing department and have them place a picture of Martin and his bio alongside our normal, full-page ad with the *New York Times*."

Hunter gripped his briefcase. "Are you sure this is the man you want to honor? I mean, he's colored."

"Martin is a hero. I don't care what he looks like. He's been loyal to me since the inception of King's. He deserves my thanks and respect. And Hunter, don't ever, ever use the word 'colored' in my presence again. I know you fired some to help the store but no one, Black or White, is as good a man as Martin."

Hunter nodded and headed back to his office. He slammed the door and pounded on his desk. To think he had to tell Martin this news personally, as well as sit through the store meeting and watch him being promoted. The whole thing was preposterous. How could he go through with this? What would his wife say? And how could he send Martin off now under the pretense of learning about security when he was an honored employee?

Hunter held his head in his hands, his mind spinning, thinking of how unfair life was. He had been born in an extremely poor family. His father left soon after and his mother was usually drunk and asleep in bed. He'd search for food from garbage cans. When he was about eight, he was sent to live with his uncle and aunt on their farm in the country. They expected him to work the fields and milk the cows alongside the colored hands. He got madder every time he saw his aunt or uncle give those people extra food or clothes. He was white! And family! He should have been given more than any of them. Hatred and bitterness filled him. He should have gotten everything growing up. He deserved to be wealthy and famous. His life would be better if he could just get rid of all those coloreds. He needed to come up with a plan.

Then the solution came to him—he would devise a way for King to sign a document that said all coloreds who were working for King would be terminated, which, of course, would include Martin. King would be the scapegoat. But more needed to be done. Hunter remembered Martin had been born and raised in Mississippi. And a Klan member talked about a black man running away with a white child years ago. Could that be Martin?

"I could contact all my buddies in the Ku Klux Klan throughout the South and have them march in each state, burning crosses, burning houses, and stringing up as many coloreds as they can find. They owe me since I'm the one who helped the Klan get to where it is now. I might not be able to kill Martin, but with this much destruction of his homeland and family, Martin would feel as if he had died. Living with this would be better than death."

He thought back to 1965 when the KKK had done such great work. Racial violence erupted in Selma, Alabama, when civil rights leader Rev. Martin Luther King Jr. and over five hundred supporters were attacked while planning a march from Selma to Montgomery to register coloreds to vote. The police violence that erupted resulted in the death of a King supporter—a white man named James Reeb.

A second attempt to march to Montgomery was again blocked by police, many of whom Hunter knew to be Klansmen also. Finally, in March, the march began with over three thousand participants under the glare of worldwide news publicity. But then the KKK, just after the march was completed, shot and killed Detroit homemaker Viola Liuzzo as she drove some marchers back to Selma.

With all this violence, Hunter and his friends thought they had really driven home the point these people should never vote. Of course, President Johnson went and signed the Voting Rights Act in August of 1965, which made it illegal to impose restrictions on federal, state, and local elections that were designed to deny the vote to blacks. But Hunter and his buddies didn't care. They would continue to do all they could to stop coloreds. They deserved more in life and felt that the coloreds were taking it all away from them.

Why can't we just have Jim Crow laws again? That's when everyone knew what side of the fence they were supposed to be on. But who cares if they were stopped a few years ago? He and his buddies had to stop coloreds now or they would gain full rights as citizens, threatening everyone else's way of life.

Hunter picked up the phone and started calling his friends in the deep South. This needed to happen soon. Then he would be done with Martin.

Hunter was so excited about his plans he didn't even mind contacting Martin. He called him on the phone, rather than talking face to face. He set up a full employee meeting for the next day and had his secretary put in a rush order for the plaque. King would do all the talking. He, himself, wasn't going to do another thing for Martin.

After work, Hunter was elated as he left the office and headed home to tell his wife and sons about the turn of events.

Zera turned pale when Hunter explained King's plan and what he, himself, planned to do to Martin and his people.

"If King honors this man, nothing you can do against his people will succeed. To continue to oppose him will be fatal to your career. Your plans could backfire on you."

Hunter shook his head. "Nothing will stop me from ridding the store of Martin and his kind. You have nothing to worry about. And remember, this will work. Luck is what happens when preparation meets opportunity."

What Hunter failed to realize was the long-festering hatred and bitterness over the years had seeped into his mind. He was becoming crazy.

After King finished talking to Hunter about honoring Martin, he decided to go home before Evie had a chance to leave for the office. How could he have been so irrational with this woman he loved with all his heart? He had promised to give his life for her, but he hadn't even let her discuss her own thoughts and opinions.

I need to ask for her forgiveness. I don't know what I was thinking.

He grabbed his coat and Evie's notebook, then raced home. Evie was just coming downstairs, still in her robe with her hair pulled back in a ponytail. Her eyes were red. She stopped when she saw King coming in the door.

"I've come to apologize." King dropped his briefcase and hurried to her. "You have every right not to forgive me, but please forgive me for losing my temper and storming out like that last night. I don't know what got into me. I shouldn't have treated you that way. Evie, I'm terribly sorry. Will you forgive me?"

Evie continued down the rest of the staircase to him, reached up, and touched his cheek. "You're my husband, forever and ever. Of course, I forgive you. But forgiving is nicer and easier when you say you're sorry." She smiled up at him. "I do know it's good to ask for forgiveness and to forgive. I hope we never forget that."

King leaned down, pulled her into his arms, and kissed her with all the passion he had.

"Perhaps we should continue this discussion in the master bedroom," she whispered.

CHAPTER SEVENTEEN

The next day, Hunter continued to work his contacts in the KKK who applauded his plan. Finally, someone was taking action for their cause. Knowing every Klan group would go out the same night at the same time all over the South convinced them something was finally being done to help them with their colored problem.

They chose Wednesday night, March 13, 1968, as the night they would begin their destruction, with plans to continue Thursday night—twenty-four hours of ruin and annihilation of these people and their homes—just one week away.

Hunter didn't think he could contain his excitement.

However, one of the older Klan's men was doubtful. "Hunter, your plan is good, but do you think you may be bringing in too many areas in the country at one time? Why not just let each district take care of this on their own? Let the destruction happen over time. That way, the police won't catch onto something big going down."

Hunter wasn't about to let an old codger get in his way. "Thanks for your concern, but my plan is perfect. I'm your superior in the Klan, so get your gang together."

Hunter was on top of the world. He couldn't wait to create havoc for all these coloreds. However, he had to sit through the staff meeting at closing time. Everyone showed up, and King was beside himself with excitement about honoring Martin. As King and his top officials stood by the microphone, Hunter chose to stand as far back as possible. It was sickening to watch.

"Thank you all for coming to this meeting," King said. "I realized the other day that one of you had done a great service to this store and to myself personally and I had failed to recognize his action. Martin Johnson, would you come up here?"

Martin raised his eyebrows, and his mouth hung open.

"This man," said King as he pointed to Martin, "prevented a plot to have me killed and for the store to be taken over. If it wasn't for Evie's excellent notetaking, I never would have remembered." King smiled at Evie who had been ecstatic when King told her he was honoring her sweet Martin.

"I don't think I ever expressed my deep appreciation for you, Martin. At this late date, I want to give you this plaque along with a check and a promotion. You are now a vice president at King's."

Everyone cheered and clapped. No one noticed Hunter turn and walk swiftly away.

The next day, Thursday, Hunter came into King's office. He had written the letter that would terminate all the coloreds at the store to look as if it were from King. Now that King just had a 'love' showing for Martin, there was no way Hunter could get King to sign this by itself. He found a solution.

"Mrs. Howard asked if I could give you these papers to sign," Hunter said to King. "She said you were expecting them."

"Yes, thank you. You can just put them on that stack. How about that ceremony yesterday? I'm still feeling good about doing that for Martin. I didn't see you. Weren't you there?"

"Of course, I was. I just had to slip out early and get home for one of my boy's birthday party. But yes, it was a great occasion."

"Just seeing Martin's eyes light up like that made my day. You need anything else?"

"Um, no, but I'd be happy to take those papers back to Mrs. Howard if you have time to sign them now."

"No, I'm fine. Thanks."

Sweat trickled down Hunter's neck. *What if King doesn't sign the fake document anytime soon? Or if he or his secretary read each page and catches the document's true meaning?* All he could do was to leave the letter there and hope for the best.

"OK, King. Have a good day." Hunter left King's office.

Hunter paced back and forth in his office. Phone calls were still coming in with added details about the raids making him feel a little better. Then an idea hit him. *Why not forge King's signature?* He could contact Evie and suggest she invite King upstairs for a break in the Tea Room. Then he could slip back into King's office and retrieve the document.

How could the firings happen without King knowing? Hunter had a document that supposedly would be signed by King, but he would have to find a way for the HR department to start firing the coloreds without anyone being the wiser, especially King. Oh, this was getting complicated, and he was running out of time.

As he considered other options, Hunter remembered the ongoing garbage strike and trash still piled up on the streets. This was a perfect week to persuade King and Evie to take a short trip to Connecticut. It was almost spring, and they had been thinking of building a second home in the country. They'd decided on Connecticut which wasn't too far from the city.

Smiling for the first time all morning, Hunter dialed Evie's extension. She answered on the second ring.

"Evie, how are you today?"

"Um, fine Hunter. How are you?"

"I was just with King, and he looked like he needed a break. Thought maybe you could convince him to go up to the Tea Room."

"Well, I guess that sounds like a good idea. I'll call him. You're sure he isn't too busy?"

"No, he just looks tired. Just looking out for my boss."

As soon as he hung up with Evie, he walked down the hall and hovered near King's office. Luckily, Mrs. Howard wasn't at her desk. He heard King's phone ring, and after a minute, heard him hang up. Hunter hid behind one of the support columns as King walked out of his office. *That was easy enough.*

As soon as the coast was clear, Hunter entered King's office, found the document, and left. Safely back in his own office, he took a deep breath and wiped his face with his handkerchief.

Hunter practiced signing King's name several times and then, with a deep breath, signed King's name on the fake letter. The first step in getting rid of Martin and his people was accomplished. Next step—convincing King and Evie to go on a vacation and then handing this over to HR. Once this was done, he could sit back and watch the carnage.

He could hardly wait.

CHAPTER EIGHTEEN

That afternoon, Hunter returned to King's office.

"Hunter! Glad to see you. Evie said you called her to convince me to take a break—exactly what I needed. Thank you. How are you so perceptive?"

Hunter laughed. "Just know what you need, sir. I've been working with you a while now and can tell when you need a break. In fact, that's why I dropped by now. Remember you told me you and Evie had been thinking of building a second home in the country? Well, with this garbage strike, there's practically no one shopping. This seems the perfect opportunity for you two to take a much-needed vacation, even if only a few days, and look for property."

"You know, that's not a bad idea—not bad at all. Traffic is certainly down in the store and the stench from all this garbage is overwhelming. I've even contacted Mayor Lindsay regarding the strike. He's going to ask the governor to call in the National Guard to clean the streets. So, maybe we will take a few days. I'll check with Evie. You all right with 'holding down the fort' here for a few days? I might try to get away even today. Not as much traffic on Thursday."

"Sounds like a plan. Just let me know." Hunter left King's office with a smile on his face. Everything was falling into place.

Around five o'clock, King stuck his head in Hunter's office.

"We're going. Evie can hardly wait to get out of town, and our agent is setting up land and homes to see. We may not come back till Wednesday or even Thursday next week. Are you sure you can put in extra hours here?"

"No problem at all. You two lovebirds go have fun, and good luck in finding either land or a great home. Just call if you need me and let me know when you'll return."

"Will do. Thanks again."

Once King and Evie were gone, Hunter felt like the weight of the world had been lifted off his shoulders. He needed time to think and keep all the balls in the air.

First, he would take the fake contract to the HR department today, so they could fire all the coloreds tomorrow before the weekend. Then Hunter only had to stay calm until next Wednesday when all hell would break loose. With Evie and King gone, his plan would go perfectly.

Hunter's phone rang constantly from people in the Klan—either the grand wizard himself or any of the hundreds of grand dragons, grand titans, and grand cyclops. One thing for sure, he couldn't have planned a better time to attack those coloreds in the South than now. People were sick of all this civil rights stuff that showed favoritism to these scum.

Hunter sat back in his desk chair and thought about the fight with Civil Rights. Throughout the 1960s, the civil rights movement had been gaining strength. Because of that, local Klan activity started building up across the South, including bombings, beatings, and shootings of black and white activists. These actions were all carried out by local Klansmen in secret and at night, but President Lyndon Johnson was outraged. In 1965, he delivered a speech publicly condemning the Klan and announcing the arrest of four Klansmen in connection with the murder of a white female civil rights worker in Alabama. Since then, the Klan had been itching to find a way to get back at them.

Hunter gave them the way. He would be a national hero in just under a week.

He picked up the signed document and headed to the HR department. He knew the head guy, Steve Wilkins, very well, so he didn't expect anyone to get too upset. After all, hiring and firing was just a normal occurrence.

As Hunter walked into the office, he saw Steve. "How's it going?"

"Not too bad. How are things on your end?"

Hunter handed him the folder with the document. "King wants to make some changes. He's already signed it."

"Thanks, I'll look at it later. And I need to ask you about that promotion for Martin. Everyone here in HR is delighted he got his much-deserved recognition. Was it your idea?"

Hunter tried to hide the shock on his face. He offered a quick smile. "Well, a mutual decision between some of the executives."

Steve nodded and then opened the folder. He pulled out the typed letter of termination. His eyebrows dropped. "What the ... Hunter, do you have any idea what this letter asks for? The termination of every colored we have working for us. This can't be for real. How do we even start dismissing that many people, and how on earth do we find their replacements? Some of these people have been working for King's since the business started. I'm going to call King myself."

Hunter quickly placed his hand on the phone. "Don't worry—probably a mistake. I'll call King myself."

As Hunter left the office, he started to shake. How was he going to pull this off? Steve was too loyal to the store to go ahead with this without personally talking to King. He walked to his office and began to pace. *What should I do? This is the first link to everything else happening. Hopefully, once they are fired, they will go back home, and since most of them are from the South, they will be at the right place at the right time by next Wednesday. I promised myself I'd get back at that Martin and all his kind, and I will!*

Then he came up with another brilliant idea. He'd forged the paper. He'd imitate King's voice! Hunter took a deep breath and called Steve in HR.

"Steve, this is King. Sorry, the connection is so bad. I'm calling from Connecticut and we have a bad storm up here. Did you get my letter from Hunter?"

"I was just going to call you. Are you sure you want to do this? I mean, this is mind-boggling. You're asking us to fire so many good people.?

"I have my reasons and plans. Go on and give them a termination letter for tomorrow. Then have your staff start looking for replacements. When I'm back home next week, I'll explain my reasons. Got to go. Storm is really bad, and I can't hear you."

Hunter hung up and breathed heavily. Was this going to work? *Steve didn't question that I was King.* He'd just have to wait.

CHAPTER NINETEEN

As Martin arrived for work, this Friday seemed just like any other day at King's. The staff arrived and went to their work areas—stock boys to the warehouse, drivers to the trucks, and sales help to the floor. And then many of the employees started getting a summons from the HR Department.

"What's going on?" they asked each other.

As Martin made his rounds, he saw his friends leaving their departments and heading up the elevator. Anna approached him.

"Mr. Martin, I just got this notice. What does it mean? I really love working here in the kitchen and don't want to be fired. This is a good job for me."

Martin read the HR notice she handed to him. "I'm just as confused as you are. Let me go with you, and we'll get this settled." But Martin sensed something evil was taking place.

By the time Martin and Anna arrived at the HR Department, there was a line out the door. People were crying and raising their voices.

Steve was trying his best to calm them but to no avail. When Steve saw Martin, he called him over. "Martin, I don't know what's going on. Read this letter." He shoved the letter from King in Martin's direction. "I'm supposed to fire all these people. What should I do? And why on earth would King want them fired?"

Martin read the letter carefully. It was total nonsense. But King had signed it. Or did he? Martin couldn't tell if the signature was real or not. "Just go on and follow through with the dismissals. I'll stay here with you and keep order."

Then Martin spoke to everyone in line. "I know you're as confused as I am. My name is on the list too." He heard everyone gasp. "Not sure why, I mean, I just got a plaque!" He laughed, hoping his little joke would lighten the mood. "However, let's just sign our dismissal papers and go home."

"Dismissal papers?" said several employees in unison. "What have we done?"

"I will figure this out and will personally get back with each one of you," Martin said. "Please don't cause a scene. Stay in line quietly. I promise I will get to the bottom of this."

Martin and Steve pointed to where each person needed to sign. Some of their hands shook as they did so. But everyone was quiet. They were too shocked and upset to talk anymore. As soon as the group left, Martin rushed to his office and called Evie."

"Evie's office, may I help you?" answered her assistant.

"This is Martin in security. I need to speak to Evie immediately."

"Oh, she isn't here. Went out of town with King yesterday to Connecticut. Do you want to leave a message, Martin?"

"Please have her call me as quickly as possible if she happens to call in. Do you have a contact phone number for her?"

"Let me see. She didn't leave any notes, but I know they're planning to stay at the Simsbury 1820 House in Hartford. Evie mentioned it because she couldn't wait to stay in such an historical and beautiful hotel. Does that help?"

"Sure does. Thank you."

As Martin called operator assistance, he was still reeling from King's letter. Soon, he was connected to the hotel operator.

"Hello, this is the Simsbury 1820 Hotel. How may I assist you?"

"Yes, hello, my name is Martin Johnson. I'm trying to reach Evie and King Freeman. Could you connect me please?"

"Oh, I'm sorry. They've already checked out."

"Checked out! What on earth for and where did they go?"

"Sir, I am not privy to our customers' reasons. I'm not sure why they have left our beautiful accommodations, nor where they went. Is there anything else I can help you with?"

"No, thank you." Martin rattled the phone into its base.

What should he do? This was an emergency like no other. Should he drive up to Connecticut and try to find her? That would be crazy. There were thousands of hotels. All he could do was go to King's office and see if he left a number with Mrs. Howard. His head throbbed from the stress. When he got there, Mrs. Howard wasn't at her desk. Hunter was.

"Hunter, do you happen to know where King and Evie are?"

Hunter looked at Martin with a scowl. "I thought you'd be gone by now. Haven't you been dismissed from King's?"

Martin felt a chill all over his body. He knew something bad was behind all these firings but now he knew who it was.

"Are you the one behind all this?"

"Not sure what you are talking about, Martin. I just know you're supposed to pack up and leave. Today. Now."

"Where is Mrs. Howard? I need to ask her something."

"I gave her the day off. With King on vacation, I felt the least I could do is give her a day off. You know, when King is away, I'm in charge." Hunter's tone sounded jubilant.

Martin stared at Hunter, then walked away. He wouldn't give Hunter an ounce of courtesy. But he *had to find Evie*. He bolted toward Evie's office and left a note by the phone that if she called in to please have her call him. Then he went back up to his office. He wasn't about to leave this store until the end of the day. He was responsible for taking care of the security and he wouldn't stop just because he'd been fired.

As Martin was contemplating what to do next, his phone rang.

"Martin, it's Leroy. So glad you answered. Bad things are brewing down here at home."

"Leroy? Good to hear from you. How's the family? And what do you mean bad things?"

Leroy sighed and his voice trembled. "There's talk going on that the Klan is going to strike soon and not just in Mississippi. All over the South. You remember Mozell who works for Mr. Thomas off Main Street?"

"Yeah."

"She was cleaning his office and saw all these notes 'bout 'next week's raid.' Then the next day, she heard him talking to some men about 'clearing them out of the South.' And that's not all. I'm getting calls or visits from many people about the same thing. I promise you—our people are scared. Something is brewing. Have you heard from anyone else?"

Martin sat down in his desk chair, gripping the phone. He looked out his office door and saw many of his friends holding boxes and crying as they left their offices.

"You're the first, but I think I know the source. Let me figure out what's going on and I'll get back to you. Tell your people to stay low and not to leave their homes."

"I'm so happy we're taking this trip," Evie said as they drove up to Connecticut on a rare, warm day so they had the top down on King's convertible. "This is the first time we've been away, just the two of us, since we celebrated our anniversary at the Plaza last month."

"Me too, sweetheart. Hunter came up with this idea. The store isn't as busy with the garbage strike still going on, so I don't think any emergency will come up this week. This is a great time to see if we want to buy land and build or buy an existing home."

"Let's see what the agent finds for us. If I see a house I fall in love with, that will be my answer."

"And you know what else I want? A dog."

"Oh, yes! You've been wanting a dog all your life. Yes, let's make sure we find a house or lot with plenty of room. I hope Princess will be ok when she has to share our attention."

They easily found the historic inn where Evie wanted to stay, and as soon as they unpacked, they had a delicious dinner in the restaurant on the premises.

Evie was the first to wake up the next morning. She looked at King and marveled at how handsome he was, even when he was asleep with his hair a mess. What a great idea to get away. They'd been able to really talk the previous night over dinner. Today would be even better because they would start looking at homes. She reached over and lightly stroked his face.

"Are you trying to wake me up, my Evie?" King asked.

"I'm sorry. You looked so good sleeping next to me I had to touch your face. Did you sleep well, or do you want to go back to sleep?"

"I'm ready to wake up and have breakfast. Have you ordered?"

"I will now. They have freshly squeezed orange juice. Want some?"

"Yes. You order and let me jump in the shower."

They ate on the small balcony overlooking the grounds—a peaceful way to start the day.

"Ok, let's look through the information our agent sent me." King opened the folder. "Here are some pictures of the land he'll show us, as well as some homes. However, I think I'm leaning toward building. I think the size of house I want will have to be built."

"How big are you thinking? This will be our second home, and we won't be here very often."

"I'd like a house with at least ten bedrooms and bathrooms, maybe a bowling alley, and, of course, an Olympic pool and tennis courts."

"What on earth for?" Evie laughed. "Why would we need to build something so big?"

"Hunter says a big house would be great for business. I've worked hard all my life and it's time I do something I want."

Evie was speechless.

"Hunter? You mean Hunter is behind this ridiculous idea of building a mega-mansion?"

"He says I must convey an image," King said. "I know a big house seems extravagant, but I could entertain important people in a place like that. Hunter says—"

"Hunter! Aren't you tired of Hunter? All he does is cause division and chaos. I still don't know what you see in him. He's out for himself and no one else, not even you!"

"Why are you so against him? He's made some wonderful changes to the store and has helped me create a vision for the future"

"Really? Give me one 'wonderful change' he's made."

"Hunter is my second in command. I can't believe you don't back me on this. I'm so tired of you complaining about him. I've had enough." King jumped up, grabbed his suitcase, and started to pack.

"Seriously? You're going to get this heated over a discussion about Hunter? What is really going on? You have always trusted and confided in me. What's happened?"

"I'm not going to stay here and argue with you anymore," he said. "I promised myself I wouldn't fight with you again. I'm leaving and going back to New York. You can either stay or go with me. I'm not in the mood to look at land or houses anymore. I know this isn't the twenties and women can vote, and I know some women even own their own businesses, but you still need to realize that I'm in charge when it comes to my store and employees."

Evie was shocked. What had gotten into him? He was acting irrational again. She decided the best action was no action. "You go on. Maybe you need time alone. I'll catch the train later. I'm sorry we're fighting, but I'm concerned with this hold Hunter has on you.

King didn't respond but finished packing and left.

Evie lay down on the bed and sobbed.

After Evie had cried it out, all she wanted to do was to get back home. She packed, took a taxi to the train station, then a train back to the city, and finally, a taxi dropped her off at home. When she walked in, she felt her nerves loosen.

"We decided to cut our trip short," she told Mrs. B, then made herself some tea and headed for the solarium to think. Thirty minutes later, she picked up the phone by her chair and called her office. Sara answered.

"I'm back in New York. Anything going on at the store I need to know about? Have the boxes from Paris arrived yet? And by the way, thanks again for standing in for me while we were gone."

"Oh, Evie, you won't believe what's happening today! Martin is trying to find you. Please call him as soon as you can."

"What on earth has happened?" Evie asked.

"So many people have been fired. Call Martin and let him explain."

As Evie hung up the phone, she felt an uneasiness settle over her. She called Martin's office. Fortunately, he answered on the first ring.

"Martin here."

"Martin, it's Evie. I just got your message. I'm back home. What has happened?"

"Am I ever glad you got my message." He went on to explain the events of the day. "I've been frantic and pacing the floor. I'm going to come over and talk to you in person. It's almost closing time, so let me make one more round of the store, and then I'll be there. All I can say right now is something bad is going down."

CHAPTER TWENTY

As Martin drove to Evie's house, he was still reeling from his earlier conversation with Leroy. Everything happening at King's and now down home couldn't be a coincidence. Everything had to originate from Hunter. But how could one man be that powerful? Or hate him and his people that much? The hatred was almost too ludicrous to imagine, but the pieces were starting to fit together like a giant puzzle, and the picture was ugly.

Evie answered the door. "Martin, I'm so glad to see you. Can I get you some tea or anything? I've got a mug in the family room. Let's talk there."

"Nothing for me. Just need to tell you what's going on."

They headed for the family room and sat down.

"We have to get to the bottom of this. Let me tell you what I found out this afternoon. I don't know if I'm going crazy or if the world is going down."

As Martin started to unravel what had happened since she left, he could see the color drain from her face.

"You mean every single colored has been fired? Even you? Why on earth would King do this?"

"That's what troubles me. The idea doesn't sound like King, but Steve in HR showed me the signed request, and Steve said he even talked to King personally yesterday but the call was cut short because of bad weather.

"Wait a minute. I was with King driving to Connecticut yesterday and eating dinner at the Inn. He never received a call, and the weather was perfect. There's no way he could have talked to Steve. Today after brunch, he said he was coming back to New York, but I haven't heard from him. Was he at the store?"

"I didn't see him. In fact, I was the last to leave. I wanted to make sure all the doors had been locked. I don't like the way this sounds."

"There's no way Steve could have talked to King unless King called from a payphone somewhere. Why would he do that? He was ... well, let's just say he wasn't in the frame of mind to call the store. Something else is going on."

"I think Hunter is behind the entire problem. Look, you know how much he hates me. He hasn't been quiet about that."

Evie nodded. "That's true."

"And people have heard him say 'he wanted to get rid of Martin and his kind.' For some reason, he's orchestrated all these firings." He paused. "I need to tell you what else is happening."

"There's *more*?"

"I got a call from a friend back home, Leroy. He and others have picked up snippets here and there that something big is going down. I think someone has gotten the KKK riled up, and they're going to come out of the woodwork, not just in Mississippi, but all over the South."

Evie put her hand over her mouth.

"Remember back in 1963 when civil rights leader Medgar Evers was gunned down in his own driveway? His wife, Myrlie, and their three small children were inside. That happened in Jackson, Mississippi, so who knows what could happen now. Evie, I'm worried, real worried."

Evie started to cry. She hung her head and sobbed. Her whole life was deteriorating right in front of her. King hated her. The store was crumbling because of these dismissals. And all her extended family from back home were in danger.

She looked up at Martin. "What should we do?"

"There is really only one course of action. I know I told you all your life to never, ever let anyone know your roots. But you're the only one who can save us."

"Me? How?"

"You're married to King, and he's the only one who can stop this. He has enough power and enough connections to call the FBI and get them down South in time to stop this."

Evie sat quietly but nodded.

"He can reverse all the firings. He'll do this 'cause he loves you. He'll stop everything once he knows your people are the target."

"Oh, Martin, I wish it were that simple. King is furious with me. I don't know where he is but even if I find him, he won't talk to me."

Martin pursed his lips, needing to get to the bottom of this as quickly as possible.

"I promised him I'd never keep any secrets from him. You know he would never trust me again once he knows I've kept a secret like this from him. Don't you see what would happen to me if I told him I'm half-black? He'd push me away and divorce me faster than I could even think. He'd never have children with me. My life would be over. I might as well be dead because his rejection would kill me. I could never tell him the truth about who I am. He could never forgive me for this deception!"

Martin looked at her for a moment and wiped the tears from her cheeks. "Have you ever wondered how and why you got to the position you're in?"

"Seem remarkable, I know. There are times I can't even believe who I'm married to and where I live."

"Listen, this is more than fate. You're married to one of the most important men in America. A little half-colored girl from the backwoods of Mississippi is now 'Queen of King's.' God's hand is in this. And do you think you'll escape if you hide here in your palace? For if you remain silent at this time, relief and help might come for us from another place, but one day, your secret will be found out. Who knows whether you have been brought to this place for such a time as this?"

Evie thought hard about what Martin said. She was at a crossroads and whatever direction she took would come with huge consequences. "Go home. Pray and fast. I'll do the same. But you're right. I must at least tell King the truth about what's happening to our people. I must try to save them. If King throws me out, he throws me out. And if my life is ruined, it's ruined.

Martin left, and Evie went upstairs to her bedroom. She called Margie, filled her in a little on what happened at the store, and asked her to come over as soon as she could.

Margie had been out of town, and when she heard about all the people who had been fired, she said, "Evie, you're not going to face this alone. I'll be over there in thirty minutes."

"I knew I could count on you. There's something else I must share with you. I'll wait till you get here but after you hear it, you might not want to be my friend after all."

"That will never happen." Margie hung up.

Evie began to sob and then she fell on her face on her bedroom floor and started to pray.

When Margie arrived, Evie, with great fear, shared her secret with her.

Margie took Evie's hands in hers. "Evie, you are my best friend and my sister forever. Nothing can come between us, especially something as silly as your background. Evie, we are all people God made in His image. Never forget that those who are in the Lord are chosen. A royal priesthood! He has called us out of darkness into His marvelous light. And He will see you through this. Now, let's start praying."

"Do you want something to eat?"

"Evie, I think we need to fast as we pray."

"Margie, you read my mind."

Hunter was delirious with joy. He stayed at the store after everyone left so he could man the phone in his office and keep up with what was going on in the South. Everything was working out. Steve believed he was King when he called. The coloreds, especially Martin, were gone from his store. In just a few days, more would be killed, and he and King would rule. Even though he was already a vice president at King's, maybe King would give him an even better title now that he had put together this elaborate plan. *Yes, that's it!* He should have a new title like chancellor or president and let King move up to CEO. All his friends and neighbors would be jealous. Although King had this crazy appreciation for Martin, he could change King's mind.

He rubbed his hands together. *"And, since King and Evie won't even get back home till maybe Wednesday, he won't have to know anything about it until it's over."*

Hunter decided to stay in his office all night and sleep on his office sofa. He hated the thought he might miss a call. Most of these calls were from some stupid hicks who didn't have a clue how to go about performing a raid. They should be grateful they had him to organize the raids. He also realized that he would have to fill in around the store until HR brought in the replacements. He didn't mind. What was a little extra work when the outcome would be so wonderful?

The next morning, Evie woke up in the same position she fell asleep in—on the floor. What a relief to finally share everything with Margie. They both had stayed on the floor, crying and praying through the night until finally, sleep overcame them.

But Evie had decided what to do during the night, and relief flooded her with strength. She still didn't know where King was but as soon as she saw him, she would tell him the truth.

As soon as she showered and dressed, she came downstairs, ready to look for King. Mrs. B was just walking through the foyer with a note in her hand.

"Morning, Miss Evie! Mr. King called and wanted you to know he's back in the city and in his office. He hopes you're doing well. But it's still early. Is everything OK?

Evie's heart jumped. King was back and left her a message as to where he was. An olive branch. This was great news. Maybe she would have a chance to talk to him after all.

"Thank you, Mrs. B, so much. I'm on my way to the store now. Not sure when we'll get home, but I'll let you know when we'll be here. Also, a lot has been happening at the store, but I'll fill you in later. Oh, and Margie spent the night and is still asleep. Could you get her some coffee and breakfast when she wakes up?"

"Oh, my pleasure. Margie is one of my favorites. But you need something to eat."

"I'm not eating anything right now. I'll explain later. But thank you for being so good to us."

All the way to the store, Evie was frantic with worry. How was she going to spring this on her husband? She didn't want to lose him, but why would he want to stay with her once he knew the truth?

At King's door, Evie took a deep breath. She didn't know if he would let her in. She hoped if he didn't want to see her, he wouldn't call security and throw her out.

She knocked on the door.

"Come in," said King, looking up from his papers. When he saw Evie, he jumped up from his desk, strode to her, and pulled her into an intense hug.

King had been distraught ever since he left Evie in Connecticut, so much so he decided to walk in the Connecticut countryside and come to grips with what was going on with his life. He had never acted the way he had these last months. He'd come to the office late last night and decided to be by himself until he could figure out how to apologize to Evie. That she came to him first shocked and pleased him.

"Oh, Evie, I'm so sorry for fighting with you. I don't know what's going on with me. Please forgive me."

Evie looked at him through tear-filled eyes. "Of course, I will. I argued, too, and I'm sorry. I know couples will have fights but please let's not have one like that again. Let's stay and work through the problem. Leaving in anger is the worst thing we could do."

"I agree. That's why I left the message with Mrs. B. I didn't know if you would ever speak to me again. I could literally kick myself for being so stubborn and stupid."

Evie nestled her head against King's shoulder.

"Is there anything I can do for you to make up for being such a jerk?" King asked.

"Um, yes there is. First, have you seen Hunter today?"

"You know, I did, early this morning. He must have slept in his office. He looked like he'd seen a ghost when he saw me. Said he had to rush off for a meeting. Why?"

"I need to talk to you about something especially important, as well as explain something about Hunter. But we need to be alone. I don't want to discuss the situation here at the office. Can we eat brunch at home this morning? I believe a good meal will make what I have to say much easier."

"Perfect. I haven't eaten anything since our brunch yesterday, and I'm starving. I still have some things to do but I can be home in, let's say, an hour or so? Does that work? By the way, everyone is acting strangely today, and I can't find Martin."

"Well, that's one of the things I want to talk to you about. Trust me on this. It's best you stay away from the staff till I talk to you, OK? And leave the store by the back exit."

"That's hard to do but OK. I'll stay in my office until I come home. I love you."

"Me too." Evie's smile was soft. "Remember that when I talk to you. OK?"

The store was quiet as Evie walked through. Being a Saturday, her secretary was out so Evie didn't have any more information on all the firings. Once in her office, she called Mrs. B. Evie knew the best way to a man's heart is through his stomach. Though that sounded a little manipulative, basic biology didn't change. King, as most men, could understand and reason better with a full stomach. She hoped this brunch would be as helpful to her as King's banquets had been a few years before.

"Mrs. B? This is Evie. I need your help. We need to pull out all the stops and cook King's favorite things for a brunch in about an hour. What can I pick up at the store for you before I head home?"

The rest of the morning was busy as Evie and Mrs. B got the brunch together. They decided on scrambled eggs with white cheddar cheese, thick-cut maple-sugar bacon, hash browns, and blueberry pancakes. Fresh squeezed orange juice and hot coffee would finish the meal.

"I tell you, Evie, no one would believe Mr. King can eat so much and stay so slim."

Evie started to laugh. "He was already eating like this when I met him. I'll set the table and then I think everything is done. Thanks for getting it started before I got home."

While Evie set the table, she started to wonder how she should start this difficult discussion. Before she could decide, King came through the door, pulled her into another hug, and she regained her confidence.

King raved about the food with every bite, saying this brunch was the best he'd ever had, even better than at the fancy Connecticut hotel.

"I'm so glad you're enjoying the meal," said Evie. She could tell he was relaxing and could feel a special electricity between them without either saying a word.

As brunch ended, she suggested taking their coffee to the family room. She loved sitting on this sofa, curled up with the cashmere throw King had given her on one of their trips. He sat next to her—a peaceful moment before the storm.

"Now, tell me what you wanted to talk about. Am I in trouble again."

"No, love. Before you react to what I'm going to say, please give me time to tell you everything. Promise?"

"I promise. What do you need to tell me?"

Evie set her coffee down on the coffee table, took a deep breath, and then looked up at his face. "Oh, King, this is so hard. I'm afraid even to start this conversation."

King grabbed her hand and motioned for her to continue. "You can tell me anything."

"Martin is my uncle."

"Yes, of course, I knew that. He took care of you when you were orphaned. I've heard you call him Uncle Martin."

"Yes, but listen. He's my *real* uncle. He's my mother's brother." Evie looked down, afraid to see his reaction.

"You're saying Martin is a real relative? If that's true, then your mother was a ... Negro?"

Evie looked up at him with tears falling from her eyes. "Yes. My mother was light-skinned too just like Martin. She fell in love with a white man, and they married. They were so young. Just seventeen."

King didn't offer a response. His face lost all expression.

"Marriage between the races was against the law in Mississippi. When the officers, who we think were KKK, found out about my parents' marriage, they hunted them down and killed them. That's when Martin took me away

in the middle of the night fearing they would also kill me."
Evie tried to read King's face, but he showed no hint of what
he was thinking.

"My father's family were very wealthy plantation
owners, and their son's death nearly killed them. I was the
only relative left, and fortunately, everything was to be left
to any child or children from their son after they died. They
died within the year of their son's death, probably from
heartbreak. He was their only child.

Still nothing from King. What is he thinking? His face still
didn't show any emotion.

"Did you ever hear about Richard and Mildred Loving?
They were newlyweds in a little town in Virginia and were
awakened in the middle of the night by the local sheriff.
Their crime? Being married. With my parents, it wasn't even
the sheriff but a bunch of hateful men who found them and
killed them." Evie stopped talking, searching for any sign
from King as to what he was thinking.

He walked to the window that overlooked the backyard
garden.

"King? I'm so sorry I never told you." Evie sobbed. "We
promised to never keep any secrets from each other, but
how could I tell you? I was terrified I'd lose you forever, and
that would kill me. And Uncle Martin made me promise to
never tell anyone, anyone at all. I never thought my secret
would come to this."

"What do you mean 'come to this'?" King turned from
the windows to look at her. "You mentioned you also had to
talk to me about Hunter. How is he involved in all of this?"

Evie took a deep breath and wiped her tears with the
back of her hand. "Hunter hates coloreds, especially Martin.
I'm sure you've heard his snide comments about Martin and
especially civil rights leaders like Martin Luther King Jr.
Well, Hunter has come up with this elaborate plan. First,
he fired all the coloreds who work at your store. That's why
the store seemed so strange to you this morning."

"How on earth could he do that without my knowledge?" King's face twisted in anger.

"By lying and forging your name. That's why he wanted us to go on vacation and why he was so shocked you were back today. He even called Steve in HR, disguised as you, when Steve balked at firing all those people. But that's not all."

He narrowed his eyes. "Go on."

"Martin thinks Hunter has contacted the KKK in some of the key Southern states, and one day soon, they will storm many of the colored neighborhoods and places of businesses. Hunter wants to destroy anything and everything that is Black and associated with Martin. He chose Mississippi first since that's Martin's home state."

King started shaking his head and pacing back and forth. He pounded his fist on the table.

Evie sat quietly, hoping his anger was directed at Hunter and not her.

He strode over to where she was sitting, then stopped in front of her, took her hands in his and pulled her up to face him. "I'm in shock over this news about Hunter. But about you? Evie, I love you and will always love you. Nothing will change that. Nothing. I don't care about your past. You are my present and my future. You are my wife, my confidante, my friend. I feel awful that you've had to hide this secret for so long." He touched her face, leaned in, and gave her a soft kiss. "You are mine now and forever. Don't ever doubt that. I understand about you keeping this a secret. Martin was trying to protect you all these years, but let's never have another secret from each other."

They held each other for a long moment while Evie silently sobbed on his shoulder and thanked him for not leaving her.

"I will never, ever leave you. Never let that thought cross your beautiful mind again. What we need to do now is put our heads together and fight back. Hunter will not win. We'll fight back."

CHAPTER TWENTY-ONE

The first thing King did was call Martin and ask him to come to the house immediately. Then he and Evie started brainstorming ways to stop Hunter's plan.

Martin arrived soon and explained the last few days. "King, Hunter became a dictator once you and Evie left for your vacation. No one could believe he was the same person you'd hired."

"I can hardly believe it myself," King said.

"Personally, I think he's really become crazy. Only a deranged person would attempt to do these things. From what I'm hearing from down South, something is going down soon."

"You know your people," King said. "What do you suggest we do?"

"I believe the first thing you might want to do is call your friends in law enforcement, especially the FBI. Get them to go down South and be on the ready when something happens. But tell them to be careful. Some of the local police are part of the KKK, and they will kill anyone who might get in the way."

"I'll call my contacts at the FBI, but you know what? I think I'll also call the governor of Mississippi. He could send some of the National Guard to help the FBI, but undercover. What do you think, Evie?"

"I think that's great, but let's turn our thoughts toward Hunter. How shall we deal with him? We want to catch him, of course, without him being the wiser. We may get him to confess if we play our cards right. If so, he could reveal the dates and times of the raids. He really thinks he's infallible, doesn't he?"

"Now that I think about it, he does. I mean, for anyone to fire all those good people without thinking about what I might say ..."

"Exactly," Evie said. "I've been thinking about him. The one thing he wants more than anything is to be seen as your number one guy. Let's invite him to dinner with just the two of us. Ply him with compliments and good wine. Over coffee, you can accuse Hunter of firing my uncle. I think once Hunter realizes he has fired a relative of your wife, he may panic and confess to whatever he has done. What do both of you think?"

King and Martin looked at each other and smiled.

Evie offered a small laugh. "Hunter will think he's really in with us or getting a promotion or something ridiculous and then we'll pounce on him. Let's pick a date right now. I want to get this going."

They decided to make the dinner for the following night, a Sunday, hoping the raid wouldn't happen on a Sunday evening.

Evie called Hunter while King and Martin listened. "Hello, Hunter?

"Speaking."

"This is Evie."

"How are you doing? I hope all is well with you and King. You two came home early from your trip."

"Yes, we're fine and glad to be back home, which is why I'm calling. King and I were talking about you and would love to have you come to our home tomorrow night for dinner. Just the three of us. Does six work for you? We could have drinks and appetizers before dinner. King has some news he wants to share with you."

"Why, sure. That sounds great. I look forward to it."

"Great! We'll see you tomorrow night at six. So glad you can come." Evie hung up the phone and the three of them smiled. The first part of the plan was in place.

King went into his home office and started calling his connections within the police and FBI, including John Williams, the governor of Mississippi, to see if he could call out the National Guard. Although Williams was pro segregation, he had complied with a federal court order to desegregate Mississippi's public schools, so King hoped he would help stop whatever might happen in the next few days. Once Williams heard what might happen in his state, he was ready to do anything necessary to stop this plan.

Martin had stayed on to help in any way he could. King called him into his office.

"Martin, come sit down so we can talk." Martin sat in one of the leather club chairs next to King's desk. "How could this have happened to our store? How do you, your friends, and your family live in this hostile environment? I feel I'm a man of the world, but I had no idea so much hate existed."

"Well, Mr. King, one thing I do know—all cruelty springs from weakness. Sometimes even living is an act of courage. My ancestors and I have been hanging on with as much hope and courage as we can muster. But yes, hate exists, and me and my kind have been battling hatred since the beginning of time. We just keep praying that one day all men will live in peace. That's what Dr. King prayed for and who knows, it might happen."

King shook his head in amazement.

Martin continued. "When good people like you and Evie stand up against evil, your action makes a statement. We sure thank you. As for your store? Once you bring back all those people who Hunter fired, the newspapers will have a field day. King's will once again be a shining star in all this darkness."

"I sure hope so."

"I also know every new beginning comes from some other beginning's end. Hunter's movement is ending, that's for sure. And with it, King's will have a new beginning."

Hunter hung up the phone and turned toward his wife, a great big smile on his face. "That was King's wife. She just invited me to dinner with just her and King. You see? I'm at the top now. He clapped his hands with glee. "They must have heard about the changes I've made at the store and want to personally thank me. I wonder what new title they'll give me."

His wife just looked at him. "I'm not so sure about that. Remember, he promoted one of his favorites—someone *you* just fired. I wouldn't get too excited until you really know what's going on. This high regard for yourself might get you in trouble."

"You don't know anything about business. I have everything under control."

That night, King and Evie stayed up until the early hours of the morning making plans. Besides King's phone calls, they needed to decide what type of dinner they would have the next night and how to go about turning on Hunter. They decided on a formal affair—the formal dining table with ivory linen tablecloth and napkins, their best porcelain china, Waterford crystal wine, water, and champagne glasses, as well as candlesticks, sterling silver flatware, a huge floral arrangement for the center of the table, and, of course, a gourmet meal.

They finally got to bed at three in the morning, exhausted from the emotional aspects of the last few days, fearing what could happen to innocent people if the raids weren't caught quickly enough.

They slept late, and after their coffee, started calling some of their favorite restaurants. Putting together this type of dinner in one day would be too difficult for Evie and Mrs. B, so they decided to call their favorite restaurants. While normally, five-star restaurants did not deliver, King was so well known, they agreed. Shrimp cocktail, lobster, beef filets, twice-stuffed potatoes, grilled asparagus, and salad with blue cheese dressing were some of the items that were promised to arrive at their home by five-thirty.

King called the Plaza and ordered a tray of their top desserts. He already had some Cuban cigars, along with a selection of the world's best wines.

As King and Evie surveyed the beautifully set table and the food on the buffet table, he said, "Dinner will be perfect. But, oh, Evie, I so hope we can get Hunter to confess or at least share some of his plans."

At six on the dot, the doorbell rang, and King went to the door himself. There was Hunter, in a ridiculous tuxedo, holding a bottle of wine, and smiling like the cheshire cat in *Alice in Wonderland*. King wasn't sure he could wait until coffee and liqueur to topple him. Holding back would take all the internal strength he had.

As the two men walked into the foyer, King hid a smile when he saw Evie floating down the staircase in a Maria Nina Ricci pale blue designer gown with silver trim. Her hair fell across her shoulders. *She's a perfect actress,* King thought. Princess walked down the steps too but the moment she saw Hunter, she fled from the room.

"Oh, Hunter! How wonderful you could come to my little dinner. I've wanted to treat you and King to a fine dinner for a while now. Please, come into the living room where we already have some appetizers for you. What would you like to drink? A cocktail, wine, or champagne?"

"King, I brought you a bottle of superb champagne, so let's start with that." Hunter handed the Dom Perignon to him.

King looked at the date on the bottle and laughed to himself. Hunter, ever pretentious, made sure he brought a very expensive bottle. "Thank you. Perfect idea. While I open it, please start enjoying the appetizers. Evie and I wanted to make sure to have all your favorites."

King poured the champagne into three glasses and handed two of them to Hunter and Evie.

"Let's make a toast. To the future." King said.

"To the future!" Hunter and Evie said.

They soon moved to the dining room where King pulled a chair out for Evie and then motioned for Hunter to sit before he sat down. A waiter in a black uniform served each person. Hunter ate until he was stuffed.

Finally, the meal was finished. Evie suggested taking the coffee to their private family room. As they found their places on the sofa and chairs, Evie began the long-awaited discussion.

"King, I wanted this time with you and Hunter because I need to share something with you that has given me and my people so much pain and sorrow."

"Evie, what are you talking about?" King asked. "I thought you were happy."

"A plan has been put into place to destroy my people, and I need your help."

"Who on earth would do such a thing?" King asked. "And when you say, 'my people,' what do you mean?"

Evie looked at Hunter and pointed to him. "This wicked man, Hunter Wallace! He fired every colored person at your store and is planning riots in the South to do all he can to kill and maim my people."

"Hunter? What's going on?" King demanded.

Hunter looked at Evie in disbelief, his eyes wide in terror.

"How ... how did ... your people ... colored ...?"

King's chair toppled when he stormed to the open patio doors where he stared into the night sky for a moment then, leaving the doors open, he strode back to his chair, his hands fisted, and glared at Hunter.

Hunter grew pale with fright. He fell to his knees before Evie and pleaded with her to spare him. "I didn't know the coloreds were your people. I didn't know what I was doing. It's all a mistake. I can fix this. I'll stop the KKK from raiding."

As Evie tried to push him away, he fell onto her lap just as King reached her chair.

"Are you going to try to rape my wife right before my eyes?" King asked.

As he finished his question, two men came into the room from the patio.

"Detectives, take this man away and send him to Mississippi. If the raids happen before we can stop them, throw him into the worst part of it. Otherwise, put him in jail. I have a feeling he will be there for an exceptionally long time."

Hunter was still on the floor by Evie, wailing in protest and trying to get away. The detectives pulled him to his feet, cuffed him, and marched him out the front door and to their car.

King and Evie, through tears, held each other close.

"I still can't believe I let a snake like that enter our lives. Oh, Evie, will you ever be able to forgive me? I promise I'll make it up to you."

"King, there's nothing you need to do. He was a master manipulator—a con man. He knew how to draw you away from the truth, so he fed you lies that sounded good. Now, let's call Martin with the good news and ask him to come over."

As soon as Martin arrived, King made a promise. "Martin, every single person Hunter fired will be hired back immediately. And you, my loyal friend, are now my executive vice president. As my right-hand man, you'll have Hunter's corner office. I know I can trust you with my life. Again."

King shook Martin's hand.

"What happened to Hunter?" Martin asked.

"I had some detectives on the patio. They heard Hunter confess to getting the KKK riled up. They contacted authorities in Mississippi, trying to stop whatever was going to happen. We don't know if we succeeded in that."

"I'll hear from my friends as soon as they know anything," Martin assured him.

"The ironic aspect of the whole affair," King said, "is that Hunter is headed down there, stuck right in the middle of the KKK and the people he wanted to harm. I can't wait to hear from the men I sent down there. I'll call them later."

Martin sat down in shock. "I still can't believe Hunter hated me and my kind so much. Evie, he didn't hurt you, did he?"

"Not at all, but I think when I told him he was attacking *my* people, he went into shock. All this time, he's been schmoozing with his perceived enemy and didn't have a clue."

They all laughed at that bit of irony.

"We appreciate you coming over, Martin. Evie and I wanted you to know exactly what's going on. If you feel you need to go to Mississippi, I'll pay for you to get there."

"Thanks, Mr. King, but I'd rather stay right here, safe and sound in New York and near Evie. It's late, so I'm going to go on home. I sure hope you two can get some sleep after all the turmoil."

"We're going to try. But first thing in the morning, meet me at my office. You and I are going straight to the HR office. We'll rehire everyone and make sure you get your new title and pay increase."

"Now you're talking." Martin laughed as they walked to the front door. "Monday can't come soon enough."

CHAPTER TWENTY-TWO

After Martin left, King got back on the phone to learn the FBI's plans. He talked with James Wilson, Senior Special Agent, who told him the best course of action at this time was no action. They could arrest more people if they waited until the raid began. All they could do is wait.

"The problem," James said to King, "is whether we can protect the people if the raids happen in multiple places at one time. Jackson, Mississippi, will be our ground zero, and from that position, we can send out police and the National Guard to some of the other key cities."

"It looks like a very complicated and dangerous event," said King. "Please keep me posted whenever anything happens."

"I promise you we will, but we also have to be very careful. If the KKK thinks we're watching them, the raid will not happen, and we won't be able to arrest them. Don't worry about Hunter. We'll keep him under guard around the clock."

"He's a real con man—don't let him talk you into letting him out for one minute."

James laughed. "He can't get to a phone or contact anyone through a window. We'll offer him a deal. If he reveals those who are in leadership in the KKK and the date of the raids, we'll reduce his sentence. But in the meantime, his living conditions are not what he's used to, for sure."

"I appreciate all you are doing, James," King assured him and hung up the phone.

The following day, James called King. "Hunter talked—a lot. Full details, so law enforcement knows where the raids will originate and who will lead the different groups. They'll send out the proper number of men to stop every raid."

"That's a load off my mind," King told him.

Hunter paced back and forth in his cell muttering to himself. "How could my perfect plan have failed? That mixed-race Evie is to blame. How could I have known King's wife was one of my enemies? And to learn she's Martin's niece!"

He punched the wall. Even the pain didn't dull his anger at Evie and King—the whole world, in fact. In a moment of clarity, he admitted he was angry mostly at himself. "Why did I run my mouth to that FBI agent? Didn't change anything for me. All my planning and scheming came to no good. Zera left me. Took my boys and all my money, stocks, and bonds. Everything in the house!"

He sat on the edge of the cot and stared at the locked door.

All he had was a future behind bars—the exact result he had planned for Martin. Death would be better than this.

King, Evie, and Martin were on edge as the next few days passed slowly. Later, James called and explained to King how they had stopped the raids.

On Wednesday, March 13, 1968, some of the FBI stationed in the Mississippi woods saw the white hoods approaching a field. Some were on horseback. They lit a cross on fire, drawing more men to a circle around the fiery madness. Some had baseball bats and others had rope. Many had large lit torches. The raids were scheduled to begin after the KKK's little song and dance that was designed to get everyone fired up. A giant mistake.

Once they left the field and started toward the black shanty homes, the law came out of the dark from every direction. Without one shot being fired, they arrested all the men and put them into paddy trucks. Not one person had been killed, and every KKK member had been arrested—there as well as in the other major cities.

"I'm telling you, King, the KKK didn't even know what hit them. And the best part? They were booked at the same jail Hunter is in. I wish you could've seen him. The men spat at him through his bars, yelling profanities. Hunter was so afraid, he hid under his thin blanket. If any of those men could get to him, he would be a dead man."

King thanked James for the information, hung up, breathed a sigh of relief, and turned to Evie and Martin. "It's finally over. The FBI stopped the raids without a single person being injured or home being destroyed. Everyone involved has been arrested."

With joyous tears glistening on her cheeks, Evie hugged them both. "I can't believe no one was killed or hung or even one house burned. God created a real miracle."

"I agree," Martin said. "Prayer works. I'm just glad it's over, and hopefully, the KKK is good and dead. I've been thinking about Hunter. He's a great example of the old proverb, 'You sow what you reap.'"

EPILOGUE

King kept his promise and that same week, everyone who had been fired was rehired, and he gave all of them a monetary bonus. He addressed all his employees, apologizing and announcing Martin's new position. A thunderous applause erupted from the room. King's Department Store was back.

As the years went by, King's Department Store continued to be the leader in its industry, concentrating on customer service and hard-to-find luxury items. Most importantly to King, they were known for the way they took care of their employees. No other store could match their salary, bonus, or other perks.

Law enforcement realized there was a real threat to the black population in the deep South, as well as other parts of the country, and resolved to stop it. And they continued to update King. Unfortunately, just a month later, Martin Luther King Jr. was shot and killed. As the country mourned, no one grieved more than King and Evie. Black fabric dressed the front doors of the store, and the day of his funeral, King's closed to honor this man who only wanted to live a life of freedom and equality. Martin Luther King had once remarked that what he wanted was, "To be able to have a decent home and school for his children, to have respect that he is a man with hopes and ambitions, and for all people, no matter who they are, to have freedom, respect, and love from others."

Evie and King vowed to spend the rest of their lives pursuing justice for others. Evie was able to incorporate her earlier plan on building Circle of Hope for the hungry and homeless in New York City, and they became so successful other cities copied the format. Circles of Hope began springing up all over the country.

Once the rich and famous saw one of their own give to others, more became involved and donated money to help the poor in America. King and Evie were able to change thousands of lives. They lived a life full of love, happiness, and joy giving to each other and others for the rest of their lives.

> *After this I looked and there before me was a great multitude that no one could count, from every nation, tribe, people, and language, standing before the throne and in front of the Lamb. They were wearing white robes and were holding palm branches in their hands. And they cried out in a loud voice, 'Salvation belongs to our God who sits on the throne and to the Lamb.* (Rev. 7:9–10 NIV)

There will come a day when every person, no matter their race or nationality, sex or religion, will stand before God.

AUTHOR'S NOTE

The story of Evangeline is a modernization of the biblical story of Esther in the Old Testament. In the biblical account, Esther was an orphan, raised by her Uncle Mordecai, and sent to the king's palace to be in a competition for his next queen. Esther's uncle, just as Evie's Uncle Martin, told her to never reveal that she was Jewish. However, once Haman came into the story and had a plan to destroy all the Jews, Mordecai urged Esther to reveal who she was to her king and to reveal Haman's evil plan. She was terrified for her life as she went before the king, because she could be killed coming into the throne room without being invited. The famous statement that Mordecai said to Esther was:

> *"Do not think that because you are in the king's house you alone of all the Jews will escape. For if you remain silent at his time, relief and deliverance for the Jews will arise from another place, but you and your father's family will perish. And who knows but that you have come to royal position for such a time as this?" (Esther 4:12–14 NIV)*

In this Old Testament story, Hamon convinced the King to sign an irreversible decree that all the Jews in the land would be killed. Hamon cast the *pur*, or lot, to pick the date, which would be eleven months later. When Esther asked the King to save her people, he had Haman killed and he made a new order. The Jews in every city had the right to assemble and protect themselves, to destroy, kill, and annihilate any armed forces of anyone who might attack them, and they could also plunder the property of their enemies. The Jews were victorious over their enemies and celebrated with the festival of Purim. Jews still celebrate this yearly festival—March 13, 1968, was when the festival of Purim fell that year.

In this story, instead of being Jewish, Evangeline is half-black, and instead of being in biblical times, this story is held in the tumultuous time of the 1960s when the civil rights movement was on the threshold of changing America. One reason I wrote this story is I want the reader to understand that every person is created in God's image, no matter his or her heritage or skin color. I hope these stories, the true one of Esther and the fictional one of Evie, inspire you to love others and be ready to defend the defenseless.

I hope and pray that one day, we can love, genuinely love, one another as we are commanded to do.

> Be completely humble and gentle; be patient, bearing with one another in love. Make every effort to keep the unity of the Spirit through the bond of peace. There is one body and one Spirit, just as you were called to one hope when you were called; one Lord, one faith, one baptism; one God and Father of all, who is over all and through all and in all. Eph 4:2–6

Before I close, I must share a life-saving truth. The God who created the heavens and earth, did send His son to earth to give us new life here and eternal life hereafter. I believe with all my heart the Bible is true and the word of God, written by men while inspired by God's Spirit.

What is a joy and a relief to understand is Christianity is not a religion, but rather a relationship with God through his son Jesus Christ. It's also the only religion where God does all the work. Other religions preach all the ways for mankind to reach God. Christianity is God doing all He can to reach us! God draws us to him by the Holy Spirit and gives us the gift of eternal life when we believe and confess our belief. If you would like to become a Christian, pray this prayer:

Dear God, I know I've done bad things in this life. But I want to have you. Your Bible says, "If we confess with our mouth that Jesus is Lord and believe in our heart God raised Him from the dead, you will be saved." (Romans 10:9-10). So God, I do confess that I want Jesus to be my Lord, and I believe in my heart you are God and you raised Jesus from the dead. Thank you God for loving me and sending Jesus to earth to forgive me of all my sins. Fill me with your Holy Spirit so I can walk in your will. Amen"

If you prayed this prayer with full sincerity, Jesus now lives in your heart! Find a Bible teaching church, other Christians to have fellowship with, read your Bible daily and pray.

I can't wait to meet you in heaven one day!

God bless you!

Lane

ABOUT THE AUTHOR

Lane P. Jordan has had a national public speaking platform for almost thirty-five years. She speaks for Mothers of Preschoolers (MOPS), Stonecroft Ministries (Christian Woman's Connection), retreats, churches, schools, and seminars. She is a best-selling author and inspirational speaker, Bible teacher, artist, recording artist, and professional life coach with American Association of Christian Counseling (AACC).

Lane's first book, *12 Steps to Becoming a More Organized Woman*, sold over 30,000 copies. She has published four other nonfiction books about organization. Her first novel, *Evangeline*, was a joy to write. During a quiet time, she felt God leading her to do a modern-day version of the book of Esther which eventually led to *Evangeline*.

Lane was born in Atlanta, Georgia, one of seven children. She enjoyed scouting, piano, gymnastics, and cheerleading. She has a degree from Georgia State

University with a major in journalism, broadcasting, and public relations. She worked for Dr. Charles Stanley as an Associate Producer for the weekly television program, *In Touch*, and was also the Editor of the First Baptist Church of Atlanta's weekly newsletter, "The Witness."

Her love for writing has extended to writing for magazines, newspapers, and children's books. She's also passionate about painting—mostly in oil with landscapes and flowers, and works in acrylic for large abstracts. A gallery in Dallas represents her.

Lane also loves the outdoors. If she isn't reading or writing, she is outside walking, hiking, playing tennis, or swimming.

Her favorite activity? Being with her husband, Scott Burday, who supports her in every way possible, and her daughters—Christi and Grace, sons-in-law Mike and Chris, stepdaughter Katie, and precious granddaughter Sara.

Lane will spend all her life and eternity thanking her Lord for saving her and giving her all these many blessings.

Made in the USA
Monee, IL
10 September 2021

76957369R10108